AUTUMN LEAVES

It's September 1939, and suddenly everyone faces an uncertain future especially the children who are evacuated from the East End of London to faraway Norfolk. Billy and Jeannie Curtis, two waifs who have had to raise themselves, are billeted in the sleepy village of Little Asham. But the evacuation is destined to have a profound effect upon them both and the troubled adults whose lives they change.

AUTUMN LEAVES

AUTUMN LEAVES

by

Janet Whitehead

Dales Large Print Books
Long Preston, North Yorkshire,
BD23 4ND, England.

British Library Cataloguing in Publication Data.

Whitehead, Janet
    Autumn leaves.

    A catalogue record of this book is
    available from the British Library

    ISBN   978-1-84262-784-6 pbk

First published in Great Britain in 2008 by www.lulu.com

Copyright © 2008 by Janet Whitehead

Cover illustration © Jill Battaglia by arrangement with
Arcangel Images

The moral right of the author has been asserted

Published in Large Print 2010 by arrangement with
Janet Whitehead, care of David Whitehead

Dales Large Print is an imprint of Library Magna Books Ltd.

Printed and bound in Great Britain by
T.J. (International) Ltd., Cornwall, PL28 8RW

For My Family

Chapter One

The Pied Piper

As soon as he opened his eyes that bright September morning, Billy Curtis thought he was going to be sick. He wasn't *ill*, exactly, just ... scared.

The previous night, his mother had suddenly announced that he and his sister were being sent away for a while. She didn't know where, exactly, and she couldn't say for how long. It was, however, something to do with the war.

There had been talk of war with Germany for months now, of course. The Germans had invaded Czechoslovakia in March, and the Italians, who shared similar dreams of conquest, had invaded Albania the following month. In May, the two countries had signed an alliance – it was called the Pact of Steel – and threatened to make Poland their next target.

Sure enough, on 31st August – just two days earlier – the Germans had rolled into Poland, and the thinking now between Britain and her allies was that war was unavoidable. That being the case the Govern-

11

ment had immediately launched Operation Pied Piper – the evacuation of all children of school-age from the inner cities.

Of course, all that was of little interest to Billy. What dominated his thoughts just then was the prospect of being packed off to some unknown location for some unspecified length of time.

Sensing his misgivings, his mother had made a half-hearted attempt to allay his fears by telling him that it was for their own safety, that there was a suspicion that the Germans might fly over Britain and drop bombs on the biggest targets, and that the children would therefore be safer in a less built-up area. But it had all been so sudden, so unexpected, and Mum herself had been so *vague*, that Billy – normally a self-reliant boy who could take care of himself – had immediately started to fret.

When his dad had disappeared several years earlier, his mother, Ada, had promised him that she would always be there for them. And she *had* been, too – at first. But over time things had changed, and after Uncle George (who wasn't his uncle at all, of course) had come to stay, he'd begun to suspect that she would prefer it if he and Jeannie were to vanish the same way their father had.

'But Mum, it's *Saturday!*' Jeannie wailed suddenly, interrupting his thoughts.

Moodily, Billy studied her across the almost bare kitchen table. At eight, Jeannie was a year younger than he, and her colouring – very blonde hair and very blue eyes – was entirely at odds with his. According to his mum, Billy had inherited his dad's unruly brown hair and hazel eyes, but since he couldn't really remember his dad too well, he'd had to take her word for it.

'I *know* it's Saturday,' their mother snapped irritably, scraping salted margarine across a slice of burnt toast, then scooting it across the table to Billy like a dealer issuing cards at a poker game. 'But that's just the way it is.'

'But we don't *have* school on Saturdays!' Jeannie protested. 'School's all locked up at the weekend!'

'Well it's not locked up *today*. An' keep your voice down. You know your Uncle George likes his lay-in on a Saturday mornin'.'

Jeannie stared down at her breakfast and began to pick idly at the dark, brittle crust, her small mouth working as she muttered indignantly to herself. Watching her, Billy read all the signs, and none of them were encouraging. Jeannie had only just found out about their 'little trip' – to use their mother's expression – and he could tell that it had put her out. Her voice had immediately taken on a very slight whine, a sure

13

indication that tears weren't far behind.

Taking pity on her, he took her free hand under the table and gave her a wink.

Although he was small for his age, Billy was much older than his nine years. But then, he'd had to be. Ever since Uncle George had moved in and claimed their mother's attention, he and Jeannie had been left to fend for themselves.

Too many times they'd lain awake at night, waiting for her to come home from one pub or another, their tummies growling peevishly because the larder had been as good as empty when they'd come in from school, and he'd learned to hate those long, agonising evenings with a vengeance.

Mum had told him once that their dad had gone away because he simply didn't want to be with them anymore, and from that moment on, Billy had harboured a secret fear that his mother would one day do the same thing herself.

Time and again he'd laid there in the darkness, promising to be a good little boy if only God would fetch Mum home safely, and then he'd wait as patiently as he could until it began to look as if his worst fear had become a reality, and that she *had* gone and left them after all.

Then, as if by magic, she would stumble into the bedroom, a swaying silhouette with the sickly sweet smell of too many gins on

14

her breath, and she'd smudge their foreheads with her scarlet lipstick and tell them how much she loved them, and though Billy had taken comfort from that at first, he'd eventually come to realise that they were just words: empty words spoken – slurred, more like – to make the speaker feel somehow less guilty.

For the plain truth of the matter was that Mum didn't really love them at all, at least not in the same way that other mums loved *their* kids. Put bluntly, they were an inconvenience to her, and she'd no doubt be happier if she were rid of them altogether.

Less than a mile away, another nine year-old boy in a dark blue mackintosh stood waiting for his mother in the narrow hallway of their little terrace house. On his back was a small knapsack, lovingly made by his mother, his name – *Peter Murray* – embroidered neatly on the buckled flap. In his hand he clutched a box from which hung a large brown label which also bore his name.

Always a perceptive child, Peter had known for some time that he would have to go away sooner or later, just as he'd known that war with Germany was inevitable. His father had told him so, sometimes at great length, and had become so convinced of the fact that he'd been among the first civilian men to enlist. But that was Tom Murray all

15

over. A hero in his son's eyes and a patriot to the core, he'd been determined to do his bit for King and country.

After his dad had gone into the army, Peter had listened carefully to as many of the news bulletins as he could, and had to admit that trouble *was* brewing. Gas-filled barrage balloons had already become a common sight on the London skyline, and the Royal Navy had recently been put on full alert to counter any attempt at invasion. The army had been mobilised, censorship had been established to prevent or at least limit any careless word or phrase from giving the enemy an advantage, the Stock Exchange had been closed down for the duration and civilian aircraft had been banned from using the skies over much of the country.

And it was only going to get worse.

Just then, Peter's mother, Evelyn, bustled out of the parlour, wearing an unbuttoned coat over her pleated floral dress. Evelyn was a dark-haired woman in her early thirties, with a longish, pleasant face and warm brown eyes that now seemed sad, though she was trying not to let it show.

'Cheer up, love,' she said, noting Peter's pensive expression.

He forced his lips to smile, even though they didn't want to.

'Got your comics?' his mother asked.

He nodded, tapping the box that hung

around his neck. The box also held a gas mask and a photograph of his mum and dad on their wedding day. In his knapsack was a change of clothes, some pyjamas and toiletries, and a packed lunch for the trip.

'Come on, then,' she said, forcing herself to sound casual and businesslike, as if they were parted from each other like this every day of the week. 'We'd better get going.'

It took them twenty minutes to walk through to Apton House School, a large Victorian building where several hundred children from the immediate area had been instructed to assemble. The journey took them through tight, cobbled streets where small brown-brick houses with low, cream-coloured window sills stood shoulder to shoulder, as if daring the Hun to do his worst.

Apton House was the biggest school in East London, and the authorities were confident that the playground would comfortably accommodate the amount of children passing through its gates over that September weekend.

What seemed like hundreds of children and a fair number of adults were already milling around both in the playground and on the pavement outside. The noise they were making was tremendous. Parked along the pavement across from the school was a convoy of green and white Regal buses. At the sight of them, Peter instinctively tightened his grip on his mother's hand.

Evelyn gave him a comforting squeeze in return. 'Don't forget, love, it'll only be for a little while,' she said, sounding more confident than she actually felt. 'And I'll visit you as often as I can.'

Peter looked up at her. He was a slim, bookish lad with short white-blond hair and gentle blue eyes. Her voice sounded a bit strange – sort of husky – and her eyes looked moist, like his did whenever he caught a cold.

'Can you see anyone you know?' she asked, surveying the crowd.

Peter peered through the open school gates. 'I think I can see Miss Turner,' he said, pointing. 'Over there in the brown coat.'

But Evelyn's attention had been taken by a poor-looking boy and girl about ten yards away, who were standing close together beside a chalk-strewn brick wall, and apparently all alone. The girl, who was about eight, was sobbing inconsolably, while the boy was doing his best to comfort her by patting her on one tiny shoulder. Both children wore their gas masks in boxes around their necks, and in his free hand the boy held a creased brown paper bag, but neither he nor the girl appeared to have any other luggage that Evelyn could see.

With a frown, she picked her way through

18

the crowd with Peter in tow. 'What's the matter, love?' she asked, finally kneeling beside the girl. She had to speak up to be heard above the surrounding babble. 'Where's mummy, eh?'

The boy looked at her, the expression on his round, dark face bleak. He wore a white shirt with a grubby, frayed collar, a threadbare green pullover and a grey blazer that looked a shade too small. 'She didn't have time to wait,' he replied. 'She had to go home and cook Uncle George's breakfast.'

Evelyn's jaw dropped for just a moment, before she recovered herself. Secretly, however, she was appalled that any mother could have left her children to fend for themselves at such a time.

Taking hold of the little girl's hand, she said, 'What's your name, poppet?'

When the little girl made no attempt to reply, the boy said, 'She's Jeannie. She's my sister.' He hesitated a moment, then added, 'I'm Billy.'

'All right, then, Billy. This is Peter. You can all keep each other company on the journey, if you like.'

At that moment a tall, thin woman looking very prim and smart in a pale blue twin-set, pushed through the crowd to join them. She was holding a clipboard to which was attached a sheaf of dog-eared papers.

'Didn't you hear me?' she asked, a disapproving look on her face. 'I said they should be with a class.'

Evelyn bristled. 'I'm sorry. We were trying to find–'

But she didn't get a chance to finish. 'We'll check their names against the list, then get them onto the bus,' said the woman in the twin-set.

Evelyn was just about to tell the woman – presumably one of the Billeting Officers she'd heard about – that Billy and Jeannie weren't really with her, when she suddenly felt Jeannie's hand tighten around hers. It occurred to her then that the children might be separated, and she didn't want that to happen. Jeannie had only just stopped crying, and Evelyn didn't think it would take much to start her off again.

Pencil poised, the Billeting Officer said, 'What are their names?'

'Murray,' said Evelyn. 'Peter Murray. And these are Billy and Jeannie.'

'Billy and Jeannie…?'

'Curtis,' supplied Billy.

'Oh, so they're not *all* your children,' said the Billeting Officer, writing down their names.

'No, I just–'

'What schools do they attend?' demanded the woman, ignoring the labels attached to the children.

'Peter goes to Hever Lane.'

'An' we come here,' growled Billy.

The woman cast him a withering look. Clearly, she believed that children should be seen and not heard. 'Well, there's no time to dally. We have a schedule to keep, you know. Come along!'

She turned on one flat heel and marched away, leaving Evelyn and the children to follow in her wake.

Tucking at the waist as best she could, Evelyn said in a half-whisper, 'Now, I want you all to stick together, do you hear me? No matter what happens, just stick together.'

'Yes, Mum,' Peter said placidly.

And then, almost before she realised it, they had reached the first of the buses and the time had come to say goodbye.

For Evelyn there was an awful sense of unreality to the moment. She couldn't even begin to imagine life without Peter. But she was going to have to get used to it, just as Peter, the poor mite, was going to have to get used to life without *her*.

Steeling herself, she let go of Jeannie's hand and hugged her son with a sudden, desperate fervour. She wanted to tell him to take care, that Mummy loved him and was proud of him, but didn't want to embarrass him in front of his new friends, and in any case couldn't trust herself to speak for any length of time just then.

'Goodbye, love,' she choked.

Peter's pale, sensitive face was unreadable. ''Bye, Mum,' he said softly. 'Look after yourself.' And then his large blue eyes dropped to the rounded bulge of her tummy and he added, 'And the baby.'

Nodding, she offered Jeannie a tremulous smile and ruffled Billy's unruly brown hair, then backed away to join the other parents and assorted adults waiting by the kerb. Some of the women in the crowd were already crying. Evelyn wanted to cry too but fought the impulse because she knew it would upset Peter.

Be strong, she told herself. *At least until he's out of sight.*

The children, meanwhile, climbed onto the bus and vanished inside. Evelyn strained to follow their silhouettes as they made their way along the vehicle. Peter sat close to one of the windows. A moment later Billy appeared next to him. Evelyn stood on tip-toe to see where Jeannie was, and caught sight of her little blonde head between the two boys.

By now everyone was waving frantically, and the last-minute calls of parents and children were being drowned by the sound of 7.7 litre Comet III diesel engines growling to life. Then, one after another, the buses finally began to pull away from the kerb.

Evelyn spotted Peter waving energetically through the window and blew him a kiss.

Let the war be over quick, she thought.

And as Peter's miserable-looking face pressed close to the window, his eyes meeting hers, she mouthed, *See you soon, love.*

And added to herself, *God willing.*

Chapter Two

Getting to Know You

They reached their destination – Liverpool Street Station – just after eight o'clock. The journey took longer than it should have due to the amount of traffic converging on the mainline station that morning.

For many of the children, who had never been on a bus before, the ride had been a complete novelty. 'Are we there already?' asked a small voice from somewhere at the back, sounding clearly disappointed.

'Don't be daft!'

'My mum said we're going on a train!' came another excited cry.

'I've never been on a bus *or* a train,' said Billy, straining to look out of the window at the vast, imposing bulk of the grubby Victorian station.

'I have,' Peter responded. 'Once. But my mum and dad were with me.'

A voice of authority piped up just then, coming from the front of the bus. A stern bark of sound, it silenced all the chattering at once.

The speaker was an official-looking man in a double-breasted navy blue suit and maroon tie. The last to board the bus, he was short and stout, with a round, red face and a small, neatly-clipped moustache. He'd introduced himself as Mr Hubbard, prompting some anonymous wag at the back of the bus to ask if he was related to Old Mother Hubbard.

'Before you leave the bus, make sure you haven't left anything behind,' instructed Mr Hubbard. 'Neither do we want any pushing or shoving as you debark! You must climb down onto the pavement and stand very quietly behind the child in front of you until you receive further instructions. Do I make myself clear?'

No child dared answer.

They clattered down off the bus, lined up as they had been told and were then led through a narrow opening and down a flight of steep steps onto an already crowded, echo-filled concourse. A number of trains were waiting at the platforms beyond the barriers, and children from other parts of the city were already piling aboard. Jeannie took hold of

Peter's hand, and though he felt uncomfortable about it, he remembered what his mother had told him *No matter what happens, just stick together.* He looked down at her and tried to smile encouragingly.

The children followed Mr Hubbard through a barrier at the far end of the concourse and onto the platform beyond. For most, it was all still a fantastic adventure. The train was like a great, segmented snake at rest, the locomotive at its head belching steam toward the station's vaulted ceiling in lively, mushrooming clouds.

'Look at that!' said Billy, having to shout to be heard above the throb and shush of the engine.

One by one, the children were ushered aboard the train. Billy, Peter and Jeannie quickly found three seats together, then watched as the carriage continued to fill with children, as many as could comfortably be squeezed in.

An adult helper had been assigned to every carriage. Mostly they were teachers from the local schools. A young woman in her early twenties was in charge of this carriage, and she was taking great care of her new charges. Of slight build, with short dark hair and a ready smile, she was quick to wipe away the tears and settle the children for the long journey ahead. She reminded Peter a little of his mum, and suddenly he had to take a deep breath to compose himself.

The teacher's shadow fell across the trio.

'Let's put your things in the luggage rack, then you'll have a bit more room,' she said. She took Peter's knapsack and reached for the old brown paper bag that was in Billy's lap. 'Where are the rest of your things?' she asked.

Billy looked up at her. 'That's it,' he said.

Letting that pass for the moment, she looked at Jeannie. 'And what about you, petal?'

'Jeannie's things are in there, too,' said Billy.

The teacher frowned. There didn't seem to be an awful lot in the bag for one child, let alone two.

'Did mummy put in a change of clothes and a packed lunch?' she asked hopefully.

'A change of clothes?' a boy's voice piped up from the seat behind them. 'A packed lunch? I thought we were only going to the seaside for a couple of hours!'

The speaker had a shock of ginger hair and was clasping a bucket, spade, and very little else. His bottom lip began to tremble.

Ignoring him, Billy said self-consciously, 'Mum was busy, so I put some things in.'

The teacher opened the bag and peered inside. It contained two bruised apples, a dry, roughly-sliced topper, three plain arrowroot biscuits, a pencil, a scrap of blank

26

paper and a dark green yo-yo.

Seeing that Billy's bag held next to nothing compared to his own, Peter whispered, 'Don't worry, Billy. You can both share with me.'

Before the teacher could pursue the matter, a piercing whistle sounded from further down the platform, followed by flurry of unintelligible cries. The train gave a shudder and a clank as the brakes were released, and the carriages began to move slowly forward. Some of the children, still beside themselves with excitement, cheered for all they were worth.

As the train picked up speed, they left the confines of the station behind them and began snaking through the backstreets of East London. Most of them were leaving the city for the first time, and the carriage was alive with chattering voices and excited shouts as the train continued to rock and sway past grimy warehouses and across ugly metal bridges.

'Where do you think we're going?' the ginger-haired boy asked no-one in particular.

'Do you think it'll be another country?' asked another.

'My mum said we're goin' to Norfolk.'

'Where's that?'

'Scotland, I think.'

'Cor!'

As the journey dragged on, and the train continued to hug the rails like a gigantic caterpillar, Jeannie fell asleep between the two boys, her head snuggled up against Billy's arm. It began to grow warm and uncomfortable, so the teacher opened a few windows. A little while later they ran into some rain, and fascinated children watched as the drops, driven by a squally breeze, scuttled slantwise across the windows.

'Is your dad goin' to fight in the war?' Billy asked Peter, as he continued gazing out of the window.

'He's already joined up,' Peter answered proudly.

'I expect that's where *our* dad is,' said Billy. 'The army.'

Peter frowned. 'I thought I heard Jeannie say you didn't *have* a dad.'

'Well...' Billy thought for a moment. 'What she meant was, we don't quite know where he is right now. *I* think he's on a secret mission for the army.'

'Really?' Peter was most impressed. 'My dad said there are a lot of secret things we don't even know about.'

'Yeah, that's right,' replied Billy. 'I think my dad must be in charge of all that, 'cause he went away ages ago and that sort of thing takes a lot of time to sort out, dunnit?'

Overhearing the conversation, the ginger boy sat forward and asked, 'Does your dad know Neville Chamberlain?'

'Probably,' said Billy.

A boy of about eight called over, 'My dad says Neville Chamberlain doesn't know his arse from his elbow.'

'Oh, he's all right,' said Billy, expansively. 'Once you get to know him.'

He sat back, pleased with himself, and wondered not for the first time exactly what his father had looked like. He'd disappeared when Billy was about two or three, so he had only the vaguest memory of him, and didn't even know his name.

An hour ticked away and some of the children began to grow fidgety. Others, including Peter, fell asleep, lulled by the motion of the train. For Billy, however, this was turning into an unexpected adventure, and he didn't want to miss a minute of it.

Eventually, finding himself at a loose end, he got up, retrieved their brown paper bag and took out the pencil and paper. With his head tilted to one side, he carefully drew a man with a stern face, thick eyebrows and a heavy moustache. Next he drew a second man, this one with a mop of hair and dark eyes, who was wagging his finger at the first man, as if telling him off.

He grinned.

It was his dad, busily teaching Neville Chamberlain the difference between his arse and his elbow.

Chapter 3

The Cattle Market

Unbeknown to the children, the train was now nearing its destination. Patchwork fields gradually gave way to farmhouses, cottages, narrow lanes and the occasional hump-backed bridge, and the locomotive itself began to slow to a crawl. Very shortly thereafter, a flower-bedecked station platform slid smoothly alongside the train.

'*Wakey, wakey!*'

The young teacher's voice cut through the expectant buzz of chatter as she worked her way along the carriage, handing each sleepy, restless or downright frightened child their bags. 'We're getting off the train now, so make sure you hold onto your things tightly! That's a very nice drawing, young man. You're quite the artist, aren't you? Make sure you put it away safely before you leave the train.'

'Yes, miss,' said Billy.

One by one the children stepped down from the carriage and formed a line along the damp platform, trying to avoid standing in the still puddles left by another recent downpour. The scene was mirrored along the entire length of the train. The sky was still heavy, but the clouds were gradually breaking to offer a glimpse of the more welcoming pale blue beyond.

'"Little Asham",' said Peter, reading the metal sign that stood next to them on the platform. 'I wonder where that is?'

Jeannie yawned and stretched. 'I'm hungry.'

But there was no time to eat just then. The children – Billy found it impossible to even guess at how many there were, all told – were led through a gateway into a narrow lane flanked by tall, small-leaved lime trees, their branches almost meeting to form a pale green canopy overhead. The damp smell of the foliage, twinned with the gloom of the lane, seemed most uninviting.

Thirty yards on, however, the trees thinned and the children found themselves back in the breaking midday sunshine. Now there were fields to left and right, occupied by a number of women workers.

One of the women, who was closer than the rest, came over to the low green-and-gold tapestry hedge and leaned on the handle of her pitchfork as they passed. She wore baggy brown breeches and a floral blouse, and her hair was pinned back under a green turban.

'Hello, you lot!' she called. 'Come to help

old Maude in the fields, have you?'

The children glanced at her, saw a pleasant-looking woman in her twenties, with a wide mouth, large teeth and lively blue eyes, but aside from the odd, shy smile, made no reply.

Up ahead the lane disappeared over a narrow bridge, and the children strained to look over the stone walls at the busy little brook that passed beneath it. At the bend, and set back from the lane, stood a small, whitewashed building in front of which stood two tall men in dark suits and a youngish woman in pumps, a long grey skirt and matching jacket.

As they approached the building, Billy tried to read the sign over the doorway. '"Vill…"' he began. '"vill…"'

'It says "Village Hall",' said the ginger-haired boy with the bucket and spade. 'Can't you read?'

''Course I can!' snapped Billy. 'It's just that the sun was in me eyes!'

The three adults came forward to meet the new arrivals and briskly ushered them inside.

The village hall turned out to be exactly that – a large, echo-filled room with a polished floor and a high ceiling, and a small ante-room off to one side where tea and sandwiches could be prepared. Long trestle tables and chairs had been stacked along one wall.

The children were told to sit cross-legged on the floor, after which one of the two men planted himself before them and said in a sharp, authoritative tone, 'This is where you are going to eat your packed lunches! You will do so quickly and quietly, and afterwards we will sort you all out with accommodation.'

Billy looked at Peter and whispered, 'Accomo-what?'

Peter smiled back. 'Somewhere to stay,' he replied.

'I hope we can all stay together,' Jeannie said in a small voice.

All around them, children were now rummaging in their bags and cases and fetching out sandwiches and fruit, while the adults huddled together in a small group, alternately chatting, then glancing around the room to ensure that order was maintained.

Billy held open his bag and studied the contents.

'Here,' said Peter. He held out a neatly-wrapped package and placed it on the floor between the three of them. 'My mum made enough sandwiches for everyone.'

Jeannie tentatively reached for a sandwich and after the first bite whispered, 'Cor. *Meat.*'

'Actually, it's spam,' said Peter, chewing

on a rather large piece. Before he could say more, however, he noticed that the ginger-haired boy, sitting nearby, looked close to tears. 'Here,' he said, and gave the boy two sandwiches.

'Thanks,' said the boy, cheering up a little. 'I *was* getting a bit peckish.'

With lunch over, the children were told to sit up straight and be quiet. Then, at a nod from the second man, the woman opened the doors to admit a steady stream of curious locals. Mostly women, they gathered on the far side of the room and examined the children with undisguised interest. The children, not surprisingly, began to fidget self-consciously.

For what seemed like an eternity there was nothing but silence broken by the odd, uncomfortable shuffle. Peter had the weirdest feeling that the whole world had come to a standstill. Then, at last, a gaunt-looking woman with black hair said, 'I'll have this one.'

All eyes turned to her choice – a boy about fourteen years old, who blushed furiously at being the centre of attention.

'He'll help me good and proper on my farm,' the woman confided to the lady standing next to her.

And so, one by one, the children were chosen by their new guardians. Perhaps, as with the first lad, they looked strong and might prove to be useful around the home. Perhaps they looked quiet and well-behaved and wouldn't be much of a burden. Some people preferred boys, others preferred girls.Younger children might take more time to settle in. Older ones would need less care.

Whatever the reason, the locals made their choices and took their charges away with them, until only Billy, Jeannie, Peter and a scattered handful of others remained.

'I don't like this,' whispered Billy.

'Neither do I,' confessed Peter. 'But we mustn't let them split us up. My mum said we've got to stick together.'

When it became obvious that the selection process had come to an end, the woman in the grey suit came over to them, offered her hand to Jeannie and said, 'come along, you three, and we'll see if anyone's got a room to spare for you.'

Nell Jackson, a short, slovenly woman who'd already made her own selection, said, 'I doubt as Gran'll turn a little 'un away, Miss Longhurst.'

The woman in the grey suit – Miss Longhurst – repeated, 'Gran?'

'Old Mrs Pearson,' explained her companion, a heavy-set woman named Norah Windom. 'Lives in the cottage a little way up on the left, just by the Green. She's already taken in one lass and her young 'uns, but I don't think she'll turn one more away. As for the other two...'

She looked down her nose at the two boys, then said, 'Why don't you try the widow-woman, her with the quiet lad she uses more like a servant? She don't go out much, so they might be company for her.'

'What's her name?' asked Miss Longhurst.

The two village women exchanged a sly, malicious glance. Then Nell Jackson said, 'Price. Beryl Price. She lives in Holly Cottage.'

Miss Longhurst nodded. 'Thank you, Mrs Jackson. Very well, children. Follow me.'

Chapter Four

For King and Country

From the outside, Holly Cottage looked like something out of a fairy tale. A low white picket fence ran along the front, broken by a slightly crooked gate. The front garden was a mass of flowering shrubs, and around the porch grew a profusion of red roses, their scent almost overwhelming in the warmth of the afternoon. A series of buff-coloured flagstones formed a path that led up to the front door, but what fascinated the children most of all was the thatched roof.

'A house with hair on!' Billy exclaimed, having never seen its like before.

Suppressing a smile, Miss Longhurst knocked at the door, then stepped back a pace. A few moments later the door was opened by a slightly chubby boy with curly black hair, who was about nine years old.

'Is your mother in?' asked Miss Longhurst.

The boy hesitated and threw an uneasy glance behind him. He had an oval face and close-set, dark blue eyes. 'She...' he began. 'She's having a lay down ... she's not very well and...'

His quiet voice drifted off into silence.

'Perhaps I can just see her for a moment,' pressed Miss Longhurst, craning her neck to see into the hallway behind the boy and the partially-open door. 'It's quite important.'

'Who is it, Edward?' called a voice from inside the house.

Seizing the initiative, Miss Longhurst stepped closer to the door and called, 'Hello, Mrs Price? May I have a quick word with you, please?'

A moment later, the door opened a little wider and a thin woman in her mid-thirties – presumably Edward's mother – appeared beside him, smoothing down her plain brown skirt. 'I'm sorry,' she murmured nervously. 'I wasn't expecting any callers.'

Miss Longhurst offered a hand. 'Hello, Mrs Price,' she said with a smile. 'I'm Cathy Longhurst, a Billeting Officer assigned to Little Asham, and I have three…'

'I'm not able to take any,' Beryl Price interrupted. 'I did explain, when they first came round. You see, I'm … not too well. I … uh … my son, Edward, has to do things for me.' She put a hand on one of the boy's shoulders and squeezed it.

'I do understand,' said Miss Longhurst, 'But I'm sure these three will be able to help you, too. They're very well behaved, as you can see.' She pulled Peter, who was the most presentable, a little closer. 'Perhaps they could stay for tonight, and we can see how you all get on?'

'Well, I don't know…' began Beryl, flustering.

'You will be doing your country a great service,' said Miss Longhurst, by way of added inducement. 'And, of course, I'm sure the money will come in handy. You'll get eight and sixpence a week for each of them.'

Still Beryl hesitated. 'It's a bit, ah, inconvenient…' she began.

'Yes,' said Miss Longhurst. 'It is. For *everyone*.'

Beryl flinched at the criticism. Her chestnut-coloured hair was brushed back off her long, pale face in a glistening roll, and

38

finger-waved at the back. Her eyes were dark, restless, her nose long and straight, her mouth a little pinched at the corners, as if it had forgotten how to relax.

'Well, perhaps just for the night, then,' she allowed at last. 'I can't say as I'll take them for any longer, mind.'

'Thank you. I'll pop back in the morning, then,' Miss Longhurst replied with a nod, and before Beryl could utter another word, she pushed all three children towards the door, turned and marched hurriedly through the gate without a backward glance.

They all stood watching her go until Beryl said, 'Well, um … I suppose you'd, ah … better come in.' She stood aside to allow the children to file past her.

They glanced around the hallway, carefully taking in their new surroundings. A grandmother clock ticked rhythmically in one corner, and a very steep staircase stood directly ahead of them. Edward was waiting uncertainly in the doorway to their right. The room into which it led was obviously the parlour, and it seemed that every available space was taken up by sturdy furniture and dainty ornaments.

'Go and put the kettle on, Edward,' said Beryl, clearly ill at ease with her new arrivals. 'I can feel a headache coming on.'

Without a word, Edward disappeared through a door at the end of the hallway, which led into the kitchen.

'You'd better leave your things here,' Beryl told the children, indicating an area beside the table. Then she walked through to the kitchen, expecting them to follow her. When they didn't, she called irritably, 'Well, come on. What are you waiting for?'

At last the children entered the kitchen, where Edward was busy spooning tea into a large brown pot. He glanced shyly at the newcomers as they followed his mother through to the scullery. There was a small Butler sink by the back door and a set of narrow wooden shelves along one wall, upon which it seemed that every imaginable kitchen utensil was kept. Beneath these there stood a table and two large Hessian sacks, one filled with potatoes, the other with little russet-coloured apples.

Beryl pointed to the sink. 'You can wash your hands here,' she instructed, looking the children up and down. Fixing her eyes on Billy and Jeannie she added, 'You two look absolutely filthy!'

She disappeared back into the kitchen, and for a few minutes the three youngsters were left alone.

'I don't like it here,' whined Jeannie, her bottom lip quivering slightly. 'I wanna go home.'

The two boys felt much the same way, but didn't see that they could really do much about it. Together they set about washing their hands in cold water. The sink was deep, and even on tip-toe Jeannie couldn't quite reach the tap. Billy had to lift her up so that the water could trickle into her hands.

Peter looked around for a towel, couldn't find one and wiped his palms down the front of his short trousers. He stood warily in the doorway, waiting for Billy and Jeannie to join him.

Edward, with his back to them, was pouring tea into five small white cups. There was no sign of his mother, and they assumed that she had returned to the parlour.

A heavy wooden table occupied the centre of the kitchen. Edward placed three cups of tea on it, then carefully carried a fourth through to his mother. He left his own cup on the counter by the teapot.

'Where are they, Edward?' they heard his mother ask. 'Tell them to come in here.'

Edward hurried back and muttered, 'You'd better come into the parlour.'

Once they had done so, Beryl looked them up and down once more, her hazel eyes lingering for a while longer on Jeannie. 'What are your names?' she asked at length.

Billy was the first to break the silence. 'I'm Billy,' he said. 'This is my sister, Jeannie.' He glanced behind him at Peter and said, 'This is Peter.'

'Peter Murray,' Peter added helpfully.

'Are you related?'

The two boys answered simultaneously.

'No,' said Peter.

'Yes,' said Billy.

Beryl eyed them askance. 'Well, are you or aren't you?'

Again their answers overlapped.

'We're brothers,' said Billy.

'We're cousins,' said Peter.

Beryl sighed, releasing air through her nose. 'What is your surname, Billy?'

'Murray,' Billy said quickly.

'Curtis,' corrected Jeannie.

Beryl nodded. This was getting them nowhere. 'Well, I'm sure I don't know where you're all going to sleep tonight,' she muttered. 'But, I suppose if it's only for one night, we can make do.'

She thought for a moment, then said, 'Edward, go and get some blankets out of my closet and make up some beds on the floor in your room.'

Wordlessly, Edward disappeared upstairs, his footfalls sounding heavy as he went from room to room, gathering what he thought would be enough to make up three beds. He knew that his mother wasn't too keen on having these children in the house, but secretly he felt rather excited at having them stay, even if it *was* for only one night.

Chapter Five

Plane Speaking

There was a comfortable silence as the three sat up at the table, alternately blowing and then sipping their tea. After a moment Edward joined them again, standing awkwardly to one side, not quite knowing what to say.

Billy came to the rescue. 'We come from London,' he volunteered.

'I've never been to London,' Edward replied. 'We've always lived in the country.' Then, changing the subject, 'Are you two brothers or cousins? You couldn't seem to make your minds up, just now.'

Billy looked at Peter, then said, 'We only met this mornin', didn't we, Peter?'

Peter nodded, stifling a yawn.

'We don't even go to the same school,' Billy continued, gazing around the kitchen.

Jeannie's eyes were slowly closing.

Suddenly there came a droning sound from outside, and the three children looked from one to the other, then to Edward, who was smiling at their expressions of alarm.

'Quick!' he said, beckoning for them to

follow him as he bolted out of the kitchen, through the scullery and out into a small, neat back garden. There, he pointed skyward, from whence the steady drone of the machine's engine was growing ever louder. Jeannie stood with her hands clasped tightly over her ears until, from over the treetops came a dark silhouette that was so low it seemed almost within arm's-reach.

The plane had a slender grey body with a sky-blue under-carriage, and each of its distinctive elliptical wings was tipped with an eye-catching red, white and blue roundel. It vanished into the distance, wagging its wings from side to side, before it disappeared over a hedge, taking the drone of its engine with it.

'Oh boy!' breathed Billy, beside himself with excitement. 'Did you see that, Peter? *Did* you?'

Peter was rooted to the spot with his mouth open. Jeannie, now wide awake and eager to share the obvious joy of her brother, started leaping up and down on the path.

Edward was amazed by the children's reaction. 'We live near one of the RAF bases,' he explained. 'They're always flying over.'

'But it … it even *waved* to us!' Peter cried enthusiastically.

'It *did* wave,' Edward agreed. 'But not to us. It was probably to the girls working out

44

in the fields.'

Billy had fallen into a thoughtful silence during the exchange. Now he said carefully, 'Why doesn't your mum want us to stay, Edward? We won't be no trouble, honest.'

Edward looked distinctly uncomfortable. 'Sometimes she doesn't ... feel well. And ... well, ever since my dad...'

He didn't finish, just looked at his feet and kicked at a small stone nearby.

'Has your daddy gone away, too?' asked Jeannie.

'Well, he died a few years ago, and ... and my mum's been a bit ... sad ... ever since,' Edward replied awkwardly.

Their buoyant mood of just moments before suddenly took a nosedive.

'I wish we *could* stay,' said Peter. 'I mean, we could all have some real larks, couldn't we?'

Edward looked up quickly, his smile revealing ever-so-slightly crooked teeth. The thought of having fun sounded fantastic, and he hoped that his mother would have a change of heart. He turned back towards the house. 'Come on,' he said. 'I'll show you where you're going to sleep.'

They all followed him back into the house, stopping abruptly when he halted in the kitchen doorway, turned to face them, put his finger up to his lips and said, *'Shhh.'*

His mother was curled up on the settee,

her head tilted back and her mouth slightly open. The children could hear her snoring quietly as they tip-toed past and headed for the stairs.

It was a steep climb to the top, where a small landing awaited them. Off the landing were three doors, two of which were slightly ajar. It was to one of these that Edward led them. He pushed the door open and then took a running jump, landing squarely in the middle of his bed, which sat in the middle of the room.

Peter followed Billy and Jeannie into the room, their eyes moving from the small wardrobe in the far corner to the chest of drawers and the large, heavy-looking trunk beside it. Edward's bed was covered in a now-dishevelled blue and white patchwork quilt. There were three windows, which made the room light and airy, each one bordered by pretty blue and white curtains. Under one window, by the side of Edward's bed, sat a pile of blankets and three pillows.

What caught the children's attention, however, was a small table that stood beside Edward's bed, and it was to this that Billy now headed.

'Cor! Where did you get these?' he asked, clearly awestruck.

Peter and Jeannie also came to have a closer look.

In the centre of the table stood a beautifully-made aeroplane. It had been made out of wood, and the detail was astounding – a sleek body with two wings set one atop the other, and with a three-blade propeller projecting from its nose. There was even a tiny pilot-figure sitting in the cockpit.

'My dad made it for me,' Edward replied proudly. 'It's a Fairey Swordfish Mark One.'

Billy pulled a face 'A *fairy!*'

'*Fairey,*' Edward repeated with greater emphasis. 'With an *e*. They've been flying since nineteen thirty-four. They can drop torpedoes or bombs, and the wings can be folded back.'

'Folded back?' asked Peter. 'Why?'

Edward shrugged. 'So that they don't take up so much space when they're in the hangar, I suppose.'

Peter grinned. 'Perhaps we'd better fold *our* wings back, then,' he decided. 'That way *we* won't take up so much space, either!'

Billy reached for the model, his eyes wide. 'Do *these* wings fold back?' he asked.

'*No!*' Edward said hurriedly. 'Be careful with it, Billy.'

Billy's hand immediately shot back. 'Well, what about these?' he asked, indicating several cruder models surrounding the bigger plane.

'*I* made those,' Edward confessed sheepishly. 'They're not very good, I'm afraid.'

'I think they're lovely,' breathed Jeannie.

47

'*Lovely?*' repeated Billy. 'I think they're bloomin' fantastic!'

'Yes, me too,' added Peter, standing with his hands clasped behind his back. He suddenly stood to attention. 'In fact,' he continued in a deep voice. 'In fact, I think we'll have these and as many more as you can make, my man. Then we'll soon win this war!'

Edward sprang up from the bed, stood to attention in front of Peter and brought his right hand up in a smart salute. 'Yes, *sir!*' he replied, and the four of them immediately fell about laughing.

When they heard Edward's mother calling from downstairs, they quickly sobered. Edward hurried out onto the landing and the others followed, pulling up sharply behind him.

'Edward,' his mother called. 'What are you doing up there?'

She sounded suspicious, and the children wondered whether their laughter had woken her.

'Come down here,' she said, without waiting for a reply. 'I want you to run an errand for me.'

Edward turned to his new companions, his quiet mood now returning. 'I won't be long,' he said. 'While I'm gone you can have another look at my models, if you like.'

The three children stood silently on the

landing for a few seconds, then wandered back into Edward's bedroom.

'Shall we make up our beds?' asked Jeannie, walking over to the pile of blankets and pillows.

'All right,' said Peter. 'It shouldn't take long.'

'Can I sleep in the middle?' said Jeannie, struggling to hold up one of the blankets with one hand while placing a pillow against the skirting board with the other.

Ignoring her, Billy wandered back to the table, still impressed by the models. 'A Fairey Swordfish Mark One,' he muttered to himself.

'I can see those ladies again!' Jeannie cried suddenly from one of the windows. 'Look!'

In the field beyond the narrow lane, more women like the ones they'd seen earlier that afternoon were working the land with hoes and pitchforks.

Billy and Peter looked out of the window above the table. Tall laurel bushes bordered the garden, beyond which stretched a small, overgrown orchard, another row of laurels and then what they took to be the village church. On the far side of the church sat a jumble of tiny cottages and various other buildings – Little Asham itself.

The window was open slightly and a warm, late afternoon breeze brought with it the rich scent of the countryside. Everything

49

seemed so quiet compared to the hustle and bustle of the London these three knew. The children stood quietly, each alone with their thoughts. Peter, feeling homesick again, took a deep breath.

All at once his thoughts were interrupted by the sound of Edward running up the stairs and entering the bedroom. Peter quickly cuffed away the single tear that ran down his cheek, anxious that no-one should see it.

'We'll be having dinner soon,' Edward announced cheerfully. Then, 'Would you like to see something else that I collect?'

He was already down on his knees in front of the large trunk and pushing back the lid.

The box was full of toys and games, and the three children quickly crowded round to see what delights it held. He took out a small tin box from which he drew a collection of long, narrow cards.

'These used to be my dad's, but now they're mine,' he said, and fanned the cards out on the floor.

'They're cigarette cards ain't they?' asked Billy.

Peter knelt beside Edward, his homesickness fading a little. '"Will's Cigarettes",' he read from the top of the cards.

The pictures on the front showed various wild animals.

'I've got a complete set of these,' Edward

explained. '*And* these,' he continued, bringing out another pack of cards bound together by a rubber band. This batch depicted a history of railway engines.

'But *these*,' said Edward, picking out another set, 'are my favourites. I don't have them all, which is a pity.'

He carefully laid out each card on the floor as if it were a ten shilling note. The children pored over them. They showed the history of aviation in fine detail.

'Hey!' gasped Peter. 'That's a picture of your model!'

'Yes, my dad made it from this very picture.' Edward held the tin upside down and a few odd cards fluttered to the floor. 'These are doubles,' he said. He glanced at the two boys and then said hesitantly, 'I was thinking. Would you two like to have these ones?'

'Oh, yes!'

'Not half!'

Peter quickly gathered up the cards. 'We can start our own collection, Billy!'

'That's not fair!' moaned Jeannie. 'What about me?'

Peter laid the cards out once more. 'All right,' he said. 'Let's see. You can have three wild animals.' He held the cards out for her to take. 'That leaves five aeroplanes and four railway engines.' He put one set in each hand, then hid them behind his back. 'You

51

choose, Billy. Left or right?'

'Left,' Billy said without hesitation. 'What have I got?'

Peter brought out his left hand and revealed the five aeroplane cards.

The smile on Billy's face spoke volumes.

Edward quickly gathered up all the cards and put them back in the tin. 'Come on,' he said. 'We'd better go downstairs. Dinner will be ready.'

They followed their newfound friend downstairs and into the kitchen, where Beryl was ladling food onto plates. She turned as the children filed in and said, 'Don't you dare sit down to eat without washing your hands first!'

The children headed for the scullery.

Chapter Six

A Guided Tour

Edward took a seat next to his mother, who indicated that Jeannie should sit at her other side. The little girl reluctantly took her place. Billy and Peter sat at the far end of the table, hardly daring to breathe for fear of upsetting Mrs Price.

Dinner looked and smelled good. It was

mashed potatoes, mince and some home-grown vegetables. Edward tucked in hungrily, so Peter followed suit. Jeannie, meanwhile, set about pushing the vegetables to the edge of her plate. She'd never liked carrots, and the other vegetables were a complete mystery to both her and Billy.

Beryl watched the girl with clear disapproval. 'Don't play with your food, young lady!' she snapped.

'But I don't like these!' wailed Jeannie, holding up a spoonful of carrots.

As always, Billy was quick to come to his sister's defence. 'We don't have anythin' like this at home.'

Edward's mother looked aghast. 'You don't have *what* at home? Carrots?'

Billy shrugged. '*Any* of it,' he replied, indicating everything on his dish.

'Well, what sort of things do you eat at home, then?' asked Beryl.

Billy thought for a moment. 'Bread an' jam, mostly,' he replied.

Beryl seemed incredulous. 'Bread and jam?' she echoed, adding, 'What sort of a meal is that?'

Billy shrugged. He didn't really know what else to say.

At the end of the meal, Beryl said, 'Collect the plates for me, Edward, and put them by the sink.' She herself rose and went to a larder cupboard, from which she took a

53

large apple pie. She set it down on the table and cut some thin wedges for each of the children. 'Pass the plates around, Edward,' she instructed, looking at each of the new arrivals in turn. 'I suppose you like apple pie?'

Billy looked uncertain. 'I don't know,' he replied honestly. 'We've never had it before, have we, Jeannie?'

The little girl shook her head. 'We like apples, though,' she said, eagerly grabbing a clean spoon.

'Well, thank goodness for *that!*' sighed Beryl.

'Can I show them around after we've finished?' Edward asked hopefully.

'I suppose so,' his mother replied. 'You can pick me some runner beans while you're out there. Take a dish with you.'

Excited by the prospect of taking a closer look at their new surroundings, the children hurriedly cleaned their plates, then raced out of the kitchen, led by Edward, who snatched up an empty bowl on his way out. Peter, however, lingered in the doorway.

'Yes?' barked Beryl.

'Thank you, Mrs Price,' the boy said quietly, and then bolted after the others.

Beryl looked towards the door, surprised by his show of manners. 'You're welcome, Peter,' she murmured before turning her attention to the dishes.

When they finally caught up with Edward, he was leaning against a tree with his arms folded.

'Your mum's quite strict, isn't she?' panted Billy.

'Do you think so?' asked Edward, sliding down the trunk until he was sitting comfortably in the shade. Without waiting for a reply he said, 'Have you *really* never had apple pie before?'

'Really,' Billy replied. 'But I must say, I wouldn't mind havin' it *again.*'

'If you *do* stay with us, you can have an apple whenever you like,' said Edward, pointing upwards.

They realised then that they were standing under an apple tree that was loaded down with small, ripe fruits.

'This is our orchard,' Edward added proudly.

The children looked around at the neat rows of small apple trees. Even to their untrained eyes, however, the orchard appeared to have been neglected in recent years, hence the amount of rotting fruits that littered the ground.

'Who picks them all?' asked Peter.

'I do. Well, sometimes my mum helps. She gives a lot to a lady in the village, but most of them end up on the ground. When I'm older, I'm going to look after it all properly.'

He jumped up suddenly, 'Come on, I'll show you what else we have!' and off he ran.

At the edge of the orchard a fence ran parallel to the road. 'That's the road into the village,' said Edward.

They walked beside the fence until it disappeared into some tall, straggly bushes.

'What are all those shiny black things on the bush?' Jeannie asked curiously. 'They're not creepy-crawlies, are they?'

'They're blackberries!' Edward said, smiling. 'Don't tell me you've never eaten a *blackberry!*'

'I haven't,' admitted Peter.

'Me neither,' said Billy.

'Here.' Edward leaned over and picked a handful, offering them to the children. 'Try one,' he said.

Jeannie wrinkled up her nose as she tentatively put one in her mouth, then just as quickly spat it out onto the ground.

Billy tried one. 'Mmm,' he managed after a moment. 'They're really sweet.' He pulled a few more off the bush and crammed them into his mouth. Purple juice ran down his chin as he chewed.

'My mum makes blackberry jam, as well,' said Edward.

Peter, who had wandered a little further on, now stood back from the bushes. 'I can see the church,' he said, shielding his eyes from the sun.

Edward came up beside him. 'Yes, the churchyard's just the other side of this hedge.'

They walked on until they came to a hole that was just big enough for them all to squeeze through. On the far side they found a forest of ancient tombstones awaiting them, broken here and there by old Celtic crosses and cherubs reaching toward the sky with tiny, weatherworn hands.

'We come here every Sunday,' Edward explained. 'Most of the village does.'

The sun was now slowly disappearing behind the church tower, but the heat of the long afternoon remained.

'I'll show you the old well,' said Edward, and they made their way back through the hedge, kicking at rotten apples as they ran to the far side of the orchard.

Here they found another natural break in the hedge where the tallest branches entwined overhead to form an arch. Beyond the arch there lay a neat vegetable garden. Edward pointed from neatly-dug rows to spindly wooden frames, identifying onions, shallots, carrots, green beans, runner beans, courgettes, broccoli and Brussels sprouts. From the surrounding borders, hyacinths, honeysuckle, orange blossom and tulips filled the early-evening air with scent.

An old well stood near the back of the vegetable garden. The four children gathered around its high perimeter wall, straining to penetrate the dark shadows at its bottom.

'I can't see anything,' said Peter. 'Is it a very long way down?'

Bracing himself on the wall, Billy hoisted himself up for a better look. 'Careful,' said Edward, grabbing him by the shirt. 'Here.'

He bent to pick up a small pebble at his feet, then dropped it into the well. The children expected to hear a splash almost immediately, but it was a good few seconds before it finally came.

'Boy, you're right, Edward,' gasped Peter. 'It is a long way down.'

'*Edward!*' came a call from the direction of the cottage.

Edward glanced that way and yelled, '*Coming!*'

To the others he said, 'I'd better get those beans. And I'll pick extras, just in case Mum lets you stay after all.'

When he'd filled the bowl, he led them all back to the cottage. Beryl was in the parlour, listening to the radio and knitting. 'Did you remember those beans?' she asked.

'I've left them in the scullery,' replied Edward.

The rhythmic *click, click, click* of the knitting needles sounded loud over the idle drone of the radio announcer's voice.

'Very well,' said Beryl. 'You can all have a glass of milk before you go to bed.' She peered at the evacuees. 'You've all fetched nightclothes, I suppose?'

Peter nodded, but Billy and Jeannie exchanged a self-conscious glance. 'We haven't,' muttered Billy.

Beryl stopped knitting and showed him a frown. 'What about a change of clothes?'

'I didn't think,' Billy apologised.

'*You–?* What about your mother?' When Billy made no reply, she gave a heavy sigh. 'Never mind. You can borrow a pair of Edward's pyjamas for tonight.' She set the knitting aside. 'Edward, go and pour the milk, and don't fill the glasses to the brim.'

The children followed Edward back out into the kitchen, where he carefully poured milk from a tall white jug into four small glasses. They took their milk and sat at the big table. Jeannie stifled a yawn and rubbed her tired eyes.

When he had finished, Edward went through to the front room, where he stood awkwardly at one end of the settee, trying to decide exactly what he should say.

'Finished already?' asked his mother, who had now resumed her knitting. 'Tomorrow, after church, I want you to take some apples up to Mrs Norman.'

'All right.'

Beryl glanced at the boy, sensing that he had something on his mind. She said, 'What is it, Edward?'

'I thought the new children could help out,' Edward suggested tentatively. 'I mean, we could pick lots more apples, there being four of us. And they were a big help to me with the beans.'

The knitting stopped again. 'Were they, indeed?' she asked sceptically. Then, 'I know what you're trying to do, Edward, but it won't work. You know I don't like company.'

He opened his mouth to argue the point, then changed his mind, for he knew his mother as well as she knew him. Head down, he sloped back into the kitchen.

A few minutes later the four children appeared in the doorway again, awaiting their next instruction, but now that Beryl had had time to think about it, she felt sorrier for the newcomers than she cared to admit. They stood fearfully in the doorway, a long way from home and among strangers. She tried to soften her tone as she said, 'I think you'd better wash your hands and faces before you go to bed.'

'Yes, Mrs Price,' said Peter. 'Goodnight.'

'Yeah,' said Billy. 'Sweet dreams.'

She offered them a rare smile and said, 'Go on, off with you.'

'I'll get you some pyjamas,' Edward said as they followed him upstairs, dragging their meagre possessions with them.

'They might be a bit big for you,' Edward

apologised as he opened a drawer in his room. He held the candy-stripe jacket up against Billy, who was at least six inches shorter than he.

Billy unbuttoned his shirt and slipped the jacket on. He giggled as he held up his arms. His hands had vanished, and the hem of the jacket came down to his knees.

Just then Edward's mother appeared in the doorway, carrying an old cotton blouse. 'Here we are, Jeannie. You can use this for tonight.' She handed the blouse to the little girl and then disappeared back downstairs.

It wasn't long before the light was switched off and they were each snuggled under the blankets, Jeannie between the two boys, her eyes already closed and her thumb in her mouth.

Supporting himself on his elbows, Peter looked across at Billy, who also appeared to be asleep, then over towards Edward. Through the gloom he could see the slow rise and fall of Edward's body under the mound of bedclothes.

He looked around the room at the un-familiar shadows now forming in the twilight, and threw back the blanket. He padded quietly over to the window by Edward's bed, held back the curtains and peered out.

'I wish I was at home now,' he breathed softly.

He gazed out into the inky blackness and

wished his mother were there to tuck him in, as she always had in the past. It was a clear night inhabited by a million twinkling stars and a bright crescent moon.

Mum'll be looking up at exactly the same sky, he thought, but curiously the knowledge didn't make him feel any better. He palmed away the tears that trickled slowly down his cheeks and did his best to stifle the sob that suddenly escaped his lips.

'Are you all right, Peter?'

Startled, he quickly turned toward the open door, where Beryl stood in silhouette.

'Uh, y-yes...' he stammered.

'Well, you don't *look* it,' she said.

He shrugged. 'Oh, I ... I think I'm getting a cold,' he replied quietly.

She hesitated for a moment, then entered the room and stepped carefully over the still forms of Billy and Jeannie.

'Come and lay down,' she said gently. 'I'll tuck you in and you'll be all safe and sound.'

Once the boy had slid back beneath the blankets, she offered him a comforting smile. 'I don't expect it will be too long before you see your mum again,' she predicted.

She looked across at Jeannie who was sound asleep, then pulled Billy's blanket up around him.

Peter watched as she walked back over to the door, turned and said quietly, 'Sleep tight.'

Chapter Seven

A Change of Plan

Sunday morning dawned bright and sunny. Not too far away, a cockerel crowed at the top of his voice, bringing Edward awake with a start.

Halfway through stretching, he suddenly remembered that he was not alone in his bedroom. He padded over to the wardrobe, pulled out his Sunday-best trousers and dressed quickly, then slipped from the room. He could hear faint sounds from downstairs, where his mother was already busying herself around the house.

Peter was the next to awake, and at first wasn't at all sure where he was. Then, remembering, he hurriedly began to dress while his companions were still asleep.

He had more or less finished when Edward reappeared, fiddling with a thin blue tie. 'Hello, Peter. I've got to go to church this morning.' He pulled a face. 'Well, I expect you'll have to go, too.'

The sound of his voice made Billy and Jeannie stir. Billy stretched and threw back the blankets. 'I dreamt I was a pilot,' he said around a jaw-cracking yawn. 'I was flying over fields and rivers. I even flew under a bridge!'

He looked down at the shirt he had put on, which was now grubby with random spots of blackberry juice.

When they got downstairs, they found Beryl busy at the range, stirring a large pot of porridge with a long wooden spoon. 'Wash yourselves and then take your places at the table,' she said. 'You'll not leave this house without some food in your tummies.'

The children exchanged glances. It was official, then. They weren't going to stay.

They were halfway through breakfast when there was a knock at the door. Beryl went to answer it.

'Good morning, Mrs Price,' came a voice they recognised as belonging to Miss Longhurst, the Billeting Officer. 'And what a glorious morning it is! How are the children? Did they settle all right last night?'

It wasn't quite so easy to catch Beryl's subdued response, so Edward snuck over to the kitchen door in order to hear what was being said. The three evacuees sat motionless, spoons in hand, their breakfast momentarily forgotten.

A moment later Miss Longhurst spoke again.

'You see, there isn't any room in the village now. All the beds are spoken for, if you get my meaning.'

Edward's mother was obviously trying to argue the point, but it seemed that Miss Longhurst had already decided the children's fate, and there was to be no changing it.

A few moments later the front door closed and Edward quickly scurried back to his chair, almost upsetting the bowl of porridge in front of him.

Beryl appeared in the doorway, looking slightly distracted. 'Well,' she said with what appeared to be a heartfelt sigh. 'It looks as if you're staying after all.'

Edward didn't think he'd ever felt happier than he did as his mother gave his crooked tie one final straighten. The sound of the church bells drifted in on the pleasant morning breeze, beckoning Little Asham's inhabitants, old and new, to worship.

'That shirt won't do, young man,' said Beryl, throwing Billy a glance that was loaded with disapproval. 'And just look at the state of your shoes!' She shook her head. 'Edward, go and fetch a clean shirt for Billy.' She inspected Jeannie. 'You'll just have to do, I'm afraid.' She took up an old hairbrush and did her best to brush the girl's matted hair.

'Ow!' cried Jeannie. 'That *hurts!*'

'I'm not a bit surprised! It looks as if it

hasn't been brushed in a week!' exclaimed Beryl.

She gradually worked the brush through the mass of blonde curls, then held the girl at arm's-length. 'That's a bit better, at least,' she decided. 'Right. If you're to stay, then we are going to set a few rules.' She looked from one child to the next, and catching Billy raising his eyebrows to Peter, said sternly, 'And there's no need to look like that, young man!'

Ignoring Billy's most angelic smile, she went on, 'We're about to go to church where I expect you all to sit still, to look and to listen. Do you understand?'

As the three children bobbed their heads, she reached for the red felt hat and brown suede gloves that were lying on the table in front of her. Then, taking Jeannie's hand, she headed for the front door, the boys following along behind.

They followed the lane back down as far as the village hall, which stood empty now, following the excitement of the previous day. A warm wind rustled the tall trees overhead, and the odd leaf fluttered ground-ward to remind them that autumn was just around the corner.

They didn't pass any more cottages, but continued walking along the gravel road, pausing once, briefly, for Peter to re-tie his shoelaces.

The bells grew louder as they approached the village green, around which clustered a few cottages and some shops, their shutters now pulled down.

The old church stood at the bottom of a long path, its round tower hinting at a rich history. A few people were already making their way up the path, mainly women in their best floral dresses, several elderly folk and a goodly number of children.

The church was almost cold enough to make Edward and his three friends shiver as they took their seats about halfway along the left-hand side of the central aisle. Beryl reached for a hymn book, as did Edward, so Peter and Billy followed suit and then sat back. The sun, shining through the arched stained-glass windows, threw splashes of red, green and gold across the heads and shoulders of the congregation.

A few moments later, the church organ groaned into life and the organist herself – a dusty old lady with grey hair – began to play a tune that was entirely unfamiliar to them.

When the piece ended, a silence that was broken only by the occasional cough or baby cry filled the building. A tall, pale-faced man of middle age, whose long black cassock identified him as the local vicar, climbed into the pulpit and welcomed the newcomers to his congregation, then spoke at length about peace and hope and the importance of thinking about absent friends and loved ones.

It was, of course, an admirable sentiment, but not one calculated to entertain children for very long. Billy, in particular, soon grew bored, put his head back as far as he could and stared up into the vaulted roof, studying its complicated network of A-frames and crossbeams.

He was halfway through another yawn when Beryl elbowed him and gave him a look that said he had better behave or else, then faced front again, listening intently to what the vicar had to say.

Billy followed suit. His interest in the sermon lasted all of ten seconds. Then he nudged Peter, and when Peter looked around at him, he crossed his eyes.

Peter suppressed a giggle.

Noticing their by-play, Edward turned toward them and mimed an exaggerated yawn, then closed his eyes and pretended to nod off.

Billy and Peter sniggered a bit too loudly, but stopped as soon as they saw Edward's mother glaring at them. She didn't look at all pleased as she grabbed Edward's arm, pulled him to his feet and seated him, none too gently, on her other side.

Billy chanced another glance at Peter, nudging him in the ribs to get his attention, but changed his mind when he found Beryl still watching him.

Then the organist struck up a lively chord and everyone rose to their feet. Peter instantly recognized the hymn. They'd sung it often enough at school, so he was able to join in without the need to consult the hymn book. As he placed his hands on the back of the pew in front, he glanced towards Edward. He too was singing, holding the hymn book out in front of him, until he sensed Peter looking in his direction. Peter gave him a wink, and Edward grinned back.

When the service was over, Beryl led the children out through the heavy wooden doors, pausing only long enough to exchange a few appreciative words with the vicar, who studied each of the children over the dark, round frames of his glasses, and then shared a good-natured joke with Edward.

It wasn't until they were out of sight of the church that Beryl stopped so suddenly that the four children bumped into one another. She pulled Edward off to one side and shook a furious finger at him. 'Don't you *dare* behave like that in church again, my lad!' she hissed.

Edward reddened.

But she wasn't finished yet. She wheeled to face Billy and Peter, who flinched at the heat in her gaze. 'Nor you two!' she said. 'I will not tolerate that sort of behaviour, do

69

you hear me?'

The boys remained silent.

'I said, "Do you hear me?"' Beryl repeated.

Peter and Billy nodded, almost afraid to open their mouths. Peter bit his bottom lip, wishing the ground would open up and swallow him. He knew his mother would be appalled if she got to hear of this.

Once again, Beryl took Jeannie by the hand and moved off down the lane at a rapid pace, the three boys following sheepishly behind.

Chapter Eight

Meet the Locals

Later that morning, the four children were sent out to the orchard to pick apples. 'We'll take the wheelbarrow,' suggested Edward. 'Then we won't have to carry them.'

They all disappeared through the arched hedge, pausing briefly to retrieve the Price's rusty old wheelbarrow, then squeaked their way through to the orchard.

'Jump in,' offered Edward. 'I'll give you a ride!'

The three children clambered into the barrow, their legs dangling over the sides. But no matter how hard he tried, Edward just couldn't lift their combined weight. Jeannie clapped her hands excitedly while the boys did their best to egg him on.

'It's no good,' said Edward at last. 'I just can't lift it. You'll have to take it in turns!'

With that, Peter and Billy jumped out, brushing bits of rust from their trousers. Jeannie sat majestically in the barrow as Edward started off at a trot, dodging the trees at the last moment and causing his tiny passenger to squeal with excitement. Billy and Peter ran off ahead with Edward in quick pursuit, over fallen branches and rotting apples, his passenger now lying in the barrow, legs in the air, laughing for all she was worth.

'Right!' called Edward, by now a little breathless. 'Whose turn now?' He tipped Jeannie out into a patch of long grass and she lay there, still giggling. Peter and Billy raced for the barrow, playfully pushing each other out of the way in order to get the next ride.

Peter won, as Billy tripped on a branch and measured his length on the mossy floor. He feigned a tantrum, hitting the ground with his fists. But Edward, complete with new passenger, immediately picked up speed and went on his way.

Jeannie yelled, *'Watch out!'*

Billy rolled out of the way, found his feet quickly and scampered after them.

After Billy and Edward had their turns, the four children regained their breath under one of the trees, where they brushed their clothes free of a mixture of rust, grass, dirt and mushy apple.

'I suppose we'd better pick some apples, then,' Edward said at last, looking up into the tree.

The branches above were laden with the fruits, which grew in clusters at the tips. Their rough skins were a mixture of red and brown.

'Make sure there aren't any holes or scars first,' Edward instructed. 'Then just give them a twist, like this.' He gently pulled on the apple and it came away easily, complete with stalk. He placed it in the barrow and then reached for another.

It didn't take long to gather the required amount, the three boys eager to climb the smaller trees in order to find the best apples. Jeannie, soon realising that she couldn't even reach the lowest branches, set off to gather some of the wild flowers growing on the mossy ground beneath the trees.

She soon had a cluster of Red Campion, their deep, rose-pink petals standing out against the subtle greens of the orchard. 'I'll take these home for Mum,' she called as she ran back, still believing that she would be reunited with her mother within a matter of days.

Edward was now heading towards the house again, wheeling the barrow with some effort, while the others followed on. 'We'll go through the side gate,' he said as they followed him through the arch and down a path at the side of the house.

Ahead, a small wooden gate led into the front garden. Billy overtook the barrow in order to lift the latch and open it wide.

'Where are we taking them, anyway?' asked Peter, as he fastened the gate behind them.

Edward stopped and put the barrow down for a short rest. 'We take them to Mrs Norman. She has a farm near the village. Then she gives us some potatoes or eggs in return,' he answered. 'I usually do it every Sunday, after church.'

He bent to pick up the barrow once again.

'Shall I take over for a bit?' offered Billy.

Edward stepped back. 'All right. Mind you keep the wheel straight, though.' And so saying, he dodged round to open the crooked front gate ahead of them, which led out onto the lane.

They made their way back toward the church again, taking it in turns to wheel the apples, Jeannie following on behind, still clutching her flowers. Halfway up the lane and almost to the church, however, they heard a sudden ringing behind them, which made them to stop and turn.

A woman rode up to them on a dark green bicycle. 'Morning, Edward!' she said cheerily. 'I see you've made some new friends.'

'Hello, Maude!' said Edward, pleased to see the woman. 'They're from London!'

'Really!' Maude replied, impressed. 'Well, fancy that!' She smiled at the children. 'Come on, then,' she said. 'What are your names?'

The trio introduced themselves.

'Well, Peter, Billy and Jeannie, I'm Maude. Maude Coker. Pleased to meet you!'

'We saw you yesterday,' said Jeannie. 'You had a pitchfork.'

'So I did!' laughed Maude.

Jeannie frowned up at her, fascinated by the brown bib-and-brace overalls the woman was wearing over her aertex shirt, and the turban that covered her hair. 'Why are you dressed like that?' she asked.

'Because it's a sort of uniform,' said Maude.

'What, like a soldier wears?' asked Billy. 'Or a copper?'

'Something like that,' replied Maude. 'I'm in the Women's Land Army.'

'What's that?' asked Billy. 'I've never heard of it.'

'Well, we'll have to educate you, then, won't we?' said Maude. And raising her voice, she sang:

'Back to the land, we must all lend a hand.
To the farms and the fields we must go.
There's a job to be done,
Though we can't fire a gun
We can still do our bit with the hoe....!'

'You're a farmer!' cried Jeannie.

'Well, we *help* the farmers,' said Maude. She reached into the long pocket of her overalls and brought out a dog-eared paper bag. 'Here, have a sweet!'

The children each helped themselves to a large chunk of coconut ice.

'This keeps me going when I'm out in the fields,' she confided. Then, winking at Peter, she noted, 'You're a quiet one, aren't you?'

Peter gave an embarrassed smile, but luckily Jeannie came to the rescue by pointing at Maude's turban. 'Have you got long hair?' she asked.

Maude pulled at the knot of the nape of her neck and shook loose a cascade of long blonde curls.

'Gosh!' said Jeannie. 'It's lovely!'

'Why, thank you,' laughed Maude. 'It's just like yours, little 'un. But I can't stand here chatting all day. There's work to be done!' Gesturing to the wheelbarrow, she said, 'I see you're off to the Normans'. Come on, Jeannie, hop on and I'll give you a ride as far as the church.'

She lifted the little girl up onto the seat of

the bicycle. 'My, there's no weight in you at all!' she noted. 'Still, a few weeks of good country living'll soon change that!'

'I won't be here that long,' said Jeannie. 'I'm goin' home to my mum probably to-morrow or the day after, and I'm goin' to give her these flowers.'

'And very nice they look, too, I must say.'

When they drew level with the church, Maude lifted the little girl down. 'This is as far as I go,' she said, hoisting herself back onto the high saddle. 'Give my regards to your mother, Edward. Hope to see you all again soon!'

The four children called their goodbyes, watching as Maude disappeared up the lane, pedalling for all she was worth.

Being a Sunday, the village was relatively quiet. In the front garden of a pastel-shaded cottage, a young mother was rocking her infant in its pram.

'That's Gran Pearson's cottage,' said Edward, nodding towards the gate.

Peter was pushing the wheelbarrow. 'Is she *your* gran?' he asked.

'No. But everyone calls her Gran,' replied Edward.

At the side gate, a homely-looking woman, her greying hair pulled tightly into a bun at the back of her head, stopped sweeping the path and looked up at the sound of her name.

'Hello, Edward,' she greeted with a cheery smile. 'And how are you this morning?'

She had a tired but kind face that had been darkened by a life spent mostly out-doors. She'd always had a soft spot for Edward, especially after losing his father the way he had. Mrs Price was a nice enough woman, too, but she did put upon the lad. He never seemed to have any friends, or time to enjoy his childhood.

'I'm fine, thank you, Gran,' Edward replied politely.

She looked at the three newcomers. 'You've got some new friends staying with you, I see,' she said. 'How's your mother, Edward? Is she keeping well?'

Edward felt comfortable with Gran. He could still remember when his mother used to visit her and Gran would bounce him on her knee, tell him stories and sing him songs. 'She hasn't been very well,' he said.

'Oh. Well, I'm sorry to hear that,' Gran replied. 'Tell her she's always welcome here for a chat and a cuppa, same as she always was.' Suddenly she held up a finger. 'Just you wait there a bit.'

She disappeared through the side gate and reappeared a few moments later carrying a cake tin. 'Here,' she said. 'A little treat for her!' She placed the tin into Edward's hands. It held a large Dundee cake sprinkled with split almonds. 'You can fetch the tin back next time you're passing, all right? There's no rush.'

Edward beamed. 'Thank you, Gran!'

He was always pleased when someone took the time and trouble to show his mother a kindness. She, like he, didn't have too many friends. She had often told him that it was because they were from another town, and village people took a long time to accept newcomers, but Edward had his own ideas. When his dad was alive, his mother always came into the village for her shopping, and was always happy to pass the time with the likes of Gran and others. But now she only ventured as far as the church on a Sunday morning, and then hurried back home before anyone had a chance to engage her in conversation.

The smell of a Sunday roast carried to them on the air, sharpening the youngsters' appetites, and with a cheery goodbye they went on their way, following the curve of the village green until they came to a lane that branched off towards the left.

'This is where I go to school,' said Edward, pointing to a small grey-stone building about forty yards further up the lane. 'We've been given another week off because of the war and everything.'

The building was old, having served generations of villagers throughout the years. A neatly-kept hedge ran along the front, separated in the middle by a tall wooden gate. Three worn steps led up to the solid oak door, and above this, *Little Asham School* had been hand-painted onto a rectangular wooden plaque.

Billy looked amazed. 'Innit small!' he said in disbelief, peering through the gate.

'Well, it's got two classrooms,' Edward said defensively.

'Our schools are a lot bigger than this, ain't they, Peter?'

Peter nodded. 'Do you have a playground?' he asked, joining Billy and Jeannie at the gate.

'We have a big field at the back,' said Edward. He led them further along the lane to a spot where the hedge finally yielded to a low wall. 'Look,' he said, pointing. 'It stretches right down towards the river.'

'How many children come here?' Peter asked curiously.

Edward thought for a moment. 'Well, there are eight in my class and five in the baby class,' he replied.

At that moment a car came around the corner and came to an abrupt halt just in front of the barrow, showering dirt and gravel in all directions. A man poked his head out of the open side window and shouted, 'Oi! Fancy leaving your wheelbarrow there!'

Edward recognised the short-cropped head of Bob Norman, Mr and Mrs Norman's son from the smallholding further up the lane, where the children had, of course, been heading. He quickly ran back to the wheelbarrow and pushed it to the side of the lane.

'Sorry, Bob,' he apologised. 'I wasn't thinking!'

Bob only grinned. He was short and skinny, with very fair hair and a bridge of freckles spanning his long nose. 'Oh, it's *you*, is it?' he said. 'The village troublemaker! Well, I won't be seeing much of you from now on, kidder. I'm joining up tomorrow!'

Edward's eyes went round. 'You're going off to fight?'

Bob paused a moment, then said, 'Haven't you heard the news?'

'What news?'

'Mr Chamberlain came on the wireless just after eleven o'clock this morning. He said that the Germans had refused to withdraw from Poland, so we were at war.'

As the children took that in, Bob patted the dashboard of his navy-blue Austin 6 and added, 'I'll have to put ol' Belle out to grass for a while.'

Bob was the only villager to own a car. It had been the talk of Little Asham when he'd first acquired it eight months earlier.

'We'll look after it for you!' offered Billy, admiring the smooth curves of the body-work.

'Oh, you *will*, will you?'

'Not half! Only charge you sixpence a week!'

'Gerraway, you cheeky mutt!'

Bob laughed and revved the engine. With a wink he sped off up the lane, turning in through the small farmyard entrance.

'It's official, then,' said Peter, thinking about his dad. 'We're at war.' He thought for a moment, then said, 'I wonder what happens now?'

By the time the children entered the Normans' yard, they could see that Belle had been parked neatly just inside a large outbuilding. Of Bob himself, however, there was no sign.

A rambling cottage stood off to their right, and Edward wheeled the barrow across to the small wooden door. When he gave the door a tap with his knuckles, a dog inside started barking, and Jeannie instinctively hid behind Billy.

'That's Rusty,' explained Edward. 'He won't hurt you.'

As the door opened, a medium-sized tan mongrel threw himself at Edward and struggled to reach his face so that he could lick it.

'*Rusty!*' called the short, stout woman who had answered the knock, and with a flick of his head the dog pushed himself away from Edward and then began to treat the other children to a few exploratory sniffs.

'I thought it might be you, Edward,' said the woman – presumably Mrs Norman. 'Come on in, all of you, and I'll get you a drink.'

The children followed Edward into a neatly-kept front room while the woman bustled around in the kitchen at the back of the property, pouring four glasses of home-made lemonade.

It was a cosy dwelling, almost Victorian in its decor, with china plates adorning the walls, alongside a host of framed photographs showing previous generations of the Norman family.

Mrs Norman came hurrying back in, carrying a tray laden with the lemonade and a plate full of fairy cakes. She had fine, curly white hair and a fresh, ruddy complexion. 'Come along,' she said as she set the tray down on a small, lace-covered table. 'Help yourselves to cake.'

The children needed no second urging.

'When you've finished, you can take the apples round to the small barn, then help yourselves to the potatoes,' the woman instructed. Studying the evacuees, she noted, 'I see Mother has a few more mouths to feed now. How is she, by the way, Edward?'

'She seems a little better today.'

'I must pop round to see her one of these days, and we'll have a little chat. You tell her that, Edward. And if there's anything I can do in the meantime, you just let me know.'

Edward nodded. Sometimes it seemed that everyone asked him the same question. *How is your mother, Edward?* But what more could he tell them? He'd grown used to telling them that she hadn't been well, but she always seemed fine to him. It was just that she didn't like to go out much any more.

As she looked down at Edward, Mrs Norman gave a hearty sigh. He was a lot like their Bob when he was that age.

'I suppose you've heard the news about the war?'

'Yes,' said Edward. 'We were just wondering what happens now?'

She shook her head. 'I dread to think, I really do. I don't know why they can't just all get together around a table and talk their differences out. Why it always has to come to war is a mystery to me.'

Edward carried the tray out to the kitchen and set it down by the sink, while Rusty sniffed around the children's feet in search of stray crumbs.

Then, with a chorus of *thank yous,* the children went back out into the mid-day sunshine and wheeled the barrow across the yard and into the small barn where the Normans kept their home-grown vegetables.

In one corner stood a pile of old wooden

crates, which they filled with the apples. That done, they then helped themselves to a pile of potatoes, and finally made their way back across the yard.

Mr Norman, a tall, pot-bellied man with fuzzy grey sideburns and a clipped moustache that was just a shade darker, was just coming out of the chicken coop, a basket over one arm. 'What about some eggs, Edward?' he called. 'Fresh-laid this morning. I can spare you half a dozen.'

'Thank you, Mr Norman.'

The man disappeared into the barn and came back a short while later holding a small box. 'Here, one of you will have to carry these!' He handed the box to Peter.

The children made their way back down the lane, through the village and home to the cottage. Edward wheeled the barrow up to the scullery door and went in to find an old sack in which to store the potatoes.

Beryl was in the kitchen, whisking batter in a large earthenware basin, when Peter wandered in to place the eggs carefully on the table. She said, 'Thank you, Peter.' And then, noticing the state of his clothes, 'Good gracious, boy! What on earth have you been doing?'

Peter looked down at his grass-covered shirt and shorts.

'Do you *all* look like that?' demanded Beryl.

'Um…'

'Well, you'll not sit down to dinner in *that* state,' Beryl declared.

A moment later the other three children put in a hesitant appearance. 'Gran sent this for you,' said Edward, hoping to placate her. He put the cake on the table beside the eggs. 'And Mrs Norman hopes to see you soon,' he added.

She set the whisk down and covered the basin with a plate. Then she said, 'Right, young man. Help me with the tin bath.' And she disappeared out into the garden with Edward following her.

On a hook in the wall hung a large bath, which they took down and placed on the flagstones just outside the scullery door. Edward's mother then began to warm pan after pan of water on the range, with which she then filled the tub.

The children stood very quietly as they watched. Surely they weren't going to have a bath out in the garden? But that was certainly the way it began to look.

'I don't quite know what you two are going to do about clothes,' she muttered, addressing Billy and Jeannie as she finally emptied a pan of cold water into the bath and tested it with the fingers of one hand. 'We'll have to sort out some of Edward's things for you, Billy, but the sooner your mother fetches some clothes up for *you*, my girl, the better.'

She disappeared once more, then came back with two large, worn towels.

'Right,' Beryl said again. 'You three take yourselves off for a walk and give Jeannie some privacy.'

Jeannie's only response was a rather pitiful, 'I wanna go home.'

When the boys returned some time later, Jeannie had not only finished her bath, but was dressed in a rather large blouse that had once belonged to Beryl. Around her waist was a length of wide blue ribbon, tied neatly in a big bow at the back. Beryl knelt by the bath, brushing the little girl's hair, another piece of blue ribbon ready in one hand.

'I don't care which of you goes next,' she said to the boys as they made to turn and disappear back indoors. 'But I'm going to make sure you each stay in this bath for at *least* ten minutes. *And,*' she added, 'mind you use the soap that's in there!'

Chapter Nine

Beside a Babbling Brook

After dinner, the children were left to make their own amusements in Edward's bedroom. They sprawled out on the floor and began to work their way through an enormous pile of books and story papers.

Although she couldn't read very well, Jeannie soon became engrossed in an old *Playbox* Annual. The book was somewhat frayed around the edges, but the illustrations quickly captured her imagination. The three boys contented themselves by flicking through Edward's comics, sharing the short stories and chuckling at the antics of the larger-than-life characters. Thus inspired, Billy soon found a scrap of paper and began to draw his own comic-strip.

Beryl had made short work of washing the children's grass-stained clothes after soaking them in the remains of the bath water, and they'd quickly dried in the warm afternoon sunshine, but she knew she couldn't do that every day until more clothes arrived for the youngsters. So, after rummaging through her wardrobe, she found a dress

87

that she no longer wore, and proceeded to cut from it two smaller dresses for Jeannie.

It had been quite a while since she'd done any dressmaking, and before she could do any now she had to oil the faithful old treadle sewing machine that had stood idle for so long in the corner of the parlour. Only then was she able to pull up a chair and begin the task of sewing the pieces together.

When she was finished, she held the dresses out at arm's-length and knew a rare moment of pleasure at the results of her handiwork.

The grandmother clock was just chiming four o'clock when there came a knock at the front door. Beryl looked up with a frown. They rarely had visitors these days, which was just how she liked it. So it was with some apprehension that she made her way to the door, one of the new dresses still in hand.

'Mrs Price?' asked the short, dark-haired woman on the front step. She was in her late twenties, with a clear, pale complexion and friendly brown eyes.

'Yes?'

'I'm Mary Roberts. I'm staying with Gran at the moment. You know, evacuated from London.'

'Oh.'

The woman offered her a small package she'd been holding. 'It's knitting wool,' she explained. 'I thought it might come in handy now that you've got some, uh, uninvited guests of your own. I fetched a load up with me, you see, and now I seem to have wool coming out of my ears.'

Beryl took the package and muttered awkwardly, 'Thank you. You're very kind.'

Her voice dried up then. She'd grown so used to her own company after Jack died that she really didn't know what else to say. But then she noticed a pram out on the street, a sunshade sheltering the baby inside it. A small, fair-haired girl of about two stood beside the pram.

Following her gaze, Mary gave a warm chuckle. 'The baby wouldn't go to sleep,' she explained, 'so I thought we'd all go for a little stroll.'

'Oh, yes. Quite.'

'That's very pretty, I must say,' Mary noticed, indicating the dress.

Beryl made a flustery, dismissive gesture. 'I'm afraid my little girl lodger hasn't fetched any clothes with her, so I've had to run this up on the machine.'

'What, you mean you *made* it?'

'Yes.'

'Gran was right, then. She said you were a clever ol' stick. Anyway, I suppose I'd better let you get on. I daresay you've got your hands full now, what with four little ones to take care of.'

89

'Oh, I'm, ah … I'm managing,' Beryl stammered. 'Would you, ah, thank Gran for the lovely cake she sent home?'

''Course. And I hope to see you again, Mrs Price. You'll have to come up for a chat.' She walked back down to the gate and took hold of the toddler's hand. 'Come on, Patsy,' she said, and released the brake on the pram.

Beryl watched her go. She was shaking. But now that she was no longer under any immediate pressure, she realised what a pleasant change it had been to chat, even briefly, to another adult.

After Jack had died so suddenly at the age of thirty-one, she'd withdrawn into herself, and after a while it had gotten so that she left the house less and less, and relied more and more on Edward to run all her errands for her. She'd always known it was wrong, of course, but she'd tried to ignore the voice of her conscience, and to an extent had succeeded.

She often told Edward that she wasn't well, that she had a headache or was tired: any odd white lie to avoid going out and mixing with people, or having to admit the truth – that she had suddenly become deathly afraid to show her face in public.

She had no idea why. The locals had shown her nothing but kindness and understanding. But Jack's death had affected her more profoundly than she'd understood. It had robbed her of her confidence and her sense of self-worth. And as a consequence she felt that she had somehow been to blame for Jack's untimely death, even though Dr Lockyer had assured her that, in the end, there had been very little that anyone could have done to prevent it.

Jack had been unwell, off and on, for years, though there had never been anything serious of specific, just a little weight-loss, some fatigue…

At first the doctor had diagnosed anaemia, and that had been a relief. But one day she'd found Jack in the orchard, clutching onto a tree for dear life, and close to passing out, and as she'd helped him back to the cottage she'd noticed an ominous blue tinge to his face that she'd never seen before.

Dr Lockyer examined him again and this time detected an irregular heartbeat. Jack was told to lead a less strenuous life, that the long hours he'd been working to try and make a go of their orchard had taken a toll on him and that he must take things a little easier. With rest and a little pinch of luck, the problem would sooner or later rectify itself.

It was only after Jack suffered a fatal heart attack four weeks later that the truth finally came to light.

He had been born with a congenital defect

which, over time, had increased the pressure on the left side of his heart. That he'd lived as long as he had, concluded the coroner, was a wonder.

With the pain of bereavement still fresh, that had been cold comfort. With Jack gone, with all their hopes and dreams gone, the light inside her went out, and she made no attempt to rekindle the flame.

But now...

Now she realised that events at home and abroad were forcing her to face life again whether she wanted to or not. The war, the children... Under these circumstances there could be no more time for self-pity. There were others to consider, now. In fact, there had *always* been others to consider, not the least of them Edward.

It wasn't going to be easy. It would take time, and she knew she would have to do it at her own cautious pace or she wouldn't be able to do it at all. But at least now she had the *will* to get better, and that was a start.

After a light tea of home-made bread and jam, plus slices of Gran's Dundee cake, the children sat at the table with Edward's mother, chatting about life back in London. They all sensed a lightening in Beryl's mood as she entertained them with stories about her own childhood, back when she had also lived in London: of how she'd met and married Edward's father, moved out to Essex, where Edward was born, then to Norfolk when he was four years old.

Edward felt a little apprehensive when the conversation began to include tales of his father. He knew from past experience that Mum usually got upset whenever she thought about Dad. But he realised now that his mother actually seemed quite *happy*, and that was a puzzle to him.

'You can write some postcards for home in a bit,' she said cheerily as she cleared the table of crockery. 'After all, your mums will want to know where you're staying and how I'm treating you all. Then Edward can show you where the postbox is, can't you, Edward?'

'Yes, Mum.'

Beryl produced a pencil and wrote her address on one side of the first postcard, along with Billy's name. 'There,' she said, offering the boy her pencil. 'Now you and Jeannie can each write a little message on it.'

Billy and Jeannie looked at each other. Neither one made any move to take the pencil.

Beryl said, 'You *can* write, can't you, Billy?'

Billy said gruffly, ''Course I can. I've just got a pain in me hand, that's all. I think I touched a stinging nettle or somethin'. It's too sore to use for writing. Maybe I'll do it tomorrow.'

He wasn't fooling her for a moment, though. 'Well, I'm sorry to hear that,' she said. 'I'll tell you what, you tell me what you want to say and I'll write it out in rough. Then you can copy it onto the postcard when your hand's not so sore.'

Billy considered that for a moment. 'All right,' he said. 'Ta.'

Peter had no such problems. Taking the second postcard, he thought for a moment, then wrote:

Dear Mum,
Arrived safely with Billy and Jeannie. We are staying with Edward and his mum. They are very nice. Please send me some more clothes. Will I see you soon?
Love from Peter xx

When the children had finished, Edward took them down to the postbox. It was really just a hole in the wall outside the station, and as they wandered back, they paused for a while on the bridge, leaning over its ancient wall in order to look down into the brook beneath.

'Are there any fish in there?' asked Billy.

'There's all sorts,' said Edward.

They looked into the distance, where the brook seemed to taper off into a thin silver line hemmed in by overhanging trees. Over to one side stood a collection of farm buildings with miniature people moving about in the surrounding fields.

All at once Edward began to unbuckle his shoes, then removed his socks. 'Come on,' he called, 'let's paddle!'

He vanished around the bridge and down to the grassy bank below, Billy, Jeannie and Peter following hard on his bare heels. Once on the bank they also removed their socks and shoes, then picked a careful path down into the water itself.

The water struck cold at first, and Jeannie screamed and curled up her toes, but it was no deeper than calf-height, and once they'd grown accustomed to the temperature, they followed Edward into the middle of the brook and then on in the direction of the distant farm.

'Hey, I just saw a fish!' yelled Peter.

'What did it look like?' asked Edward.

'It was silver, and its fins were all red.'

'That's a rudd,' explained Edward. 'See if you can spot a stickleback!'

Billy was so intent on finding one that he stumbled on the pebbly stream-bottom and had to grab Peter's arm to keep from falling. '*There's one!*' he cried.

Edward splashed over. 'Where?'

'*There!*'

Jeannie splashed up beside him. 'I see it!' she squealed.

'You clot,' said Edward, as the creature

95

vanished into the undergrowth that fringed the bank. 'That's a water vole!'

Billy frowned. 'Is there much difference?'

On they went. Edward pointed to patches of dark green crowfoot and thick, floating mats of starwort and there they found water spiders, tadpoles, dragonflies and even small whorl snails. A little further on Edward drew their attention to what he called a lamprey, a fish that didn't have any jaw.

Peter frowned. 'How does he eat, then?'

'He sucks,' Edward explained. 'He picks up all the little stones and sucks all the goodness off them.'

'Yuk!'

A few yards further on, Billy finally tripped on a small rock and went down, taking Peter with him. Disturbed fish and insects quickly scattered to every point of the compass, and Jeannie screamed as the displaced water soaked her from head to foot. Edward, who was out of range, looked on in horror.

'You're for it now!' he warned.

'It was an accident!' said Billy.

'Try telling my mum that!'

'*Right!*' yelled Peter, pushing to his feet. 'If *we're* for it, *you're* for it as well, Edward!'

'*No!*'

But Peter was already kicking water at him, and it wasn't long before Billy joined in. Soon all four were soaked to the skin, and the happiest that they'd ever been.

Afterwards, they sat on the grassy bank, hoping to dry out in the warm sunshine, but knew they couldn't stay there indefinitely.

'We'd better be getting back,' Edward said at last, pulling on his socks. He saw Billy struggling with his shoelaces and said, 'Would you like me to do those?'

Billy flexed his hands again and tutted. 'Bloomin' stinging nettles,' he grumbled. 'Can't seem to do anythin' today.'

'Can you tie mine as well, Edward?' asked Jeannie.

'Here, I'll do yours,' said Peter. 'Hold your foot out.'

When they reached the cottage, Beryl was changing the furniture around in the parlour. Although he made no comment, Edward was more than a little surprised. On the small table, which now stood in the centre of the room, was a vase full of bright yellow chrysanthemums, gathered that afternoon from the front garden. A shelved alcove next to the fireplace that was usually covered by a long curtain had been unveiled to show off a fine display of ornaments. And on the settee, folded into three neat piles, was a selection of clothes for the new-comers, including the two dresses Beryl had made for Jeannie. There were cardigans that no longer fitted Edward, and some shirts and shorts for Billy. Beryl had even sorted out some extras for Peter, at least until his own clothes arrived.

That evening, when the four of them were sprawled out in bed and the conversation had turned to stories of home and school, Peter began to feel homesick again. He missed his mother and father and everything else he knew and loved. But tonight it was Jeannie who seemed to find separation especially hard.

No matter what they did to pacify her, the little girl didn't seem able to stop crying, and eventually Edward leapt out of bed and headed for the door. 'I'll get Mum,' he said.

Beryl was listening to the wireless when Edward padded into the parlour. An announcer was just saying that France, Australia and Nepal had joined Britain in declaring war on Germany, while Egypt had declared a state of martial law in order to deport all German citizens.

Beryl looked up from the knitting patterns she'd been sorting through and said, 'Edward? Are you all right, sweetheart?'

'Jeannie won't stop crying,' he answered worriedly. 'I think she misses her mummy.'

Beryl set the patterns aside. 'Well,' she muttered, 'we can't have that, can we?'

Jeannie's face was bright scarlet and her cheeks were wet with tears when Beryl entered the bedroom. She bent down and gathered the little girl up in her arms. 'Come on, Jeannie,' she said, gently stroking the child's blonde hair. 'Let's go downstairs for a while, shall we? You can help me sort out all my knitting patterns.'

Jeannie, not trusting herself to speak, just nodded.

It was dark outside, and the three boys decided to tell each other ghost stories as they stretched out in their beds.

'If you walk just a bit further up the lane, you come to the ruins of an old abbey,' said Edward quietly. 'They say it's haunted by the ghost of a monk.'

Billy and Peter exchanged a wide-eyed glance.

'Do you think it's true?' asked Peter, not completely sure he wanted to hear the answer.

'I *know* it's true,' said Edward. 'He's been seen often enough by the people in the village. I've even seen him myself!'

Billy sat bolt upright. 'You've *seen* him?' he repeated. 'Blimey!'

Edward nodded through the gloom. 'It was a few months ago, and I'd cycled up to the old mill in Fenby. It was already getting dark by the time I got back.'

'Go on,' said Billy impatiently.

'Well, I could see the abbey from the lane, so I stopped for a minute and climbed up onto the stile just to catch my breath and get

99

a better view. That's when I saw it!'

'Saw what?' Peter asked nervously.

'A tall figure dressed in a long grey robe, standing on the abbey steps.'

Peter swallowed loudly. 'What, ah, did you do?'

'Well, I very nearly fell off the stile!' Edward replied with a grin. 'Then I got back on my bike and pedalled off down the lane for all I was worth, and didn't stop again till I'd reached home.'

Peter whistled quietly and pulled the blanket up to his chin.

'Could we go and see it for ourselves?' asked Billy.

Edward considered the idea. 'I could take you there tomorrow, if you like,' he offered.

'No,' said Billy. 'I mean *tonight!*'

'What?'

'What about Jeannie?' Peter said anxiously, hoping Edward would think it was a bad idea.

'Well, we could wait until she was asleep, then creep out!'

Edward frowned. 'We'd have to wait till my mum went to bed as well,' he mused. 'Sometimes that's not until late.'

'Well, let's put our clothes on over our pyjamas, an' then we can sneak out as soon as it's all quiet. What do you reckon?'

'What do *you* think, Peter?' asked Edward, hoping that Peter would be the one to

100

chicken out.

But rather than let them know how much the idea scared him, Peter said simply, 'All right – we'll do it!'

Chapter Ten

Ghosts in the Night

The cottage was as quiet as a tomb as the boys tip-toed slowly downstairs, stopping at every tell-tale creak before moving stealthily on.

Five steps from the bottom the boys stopped as one when a sound from upstairs drew their attention, and they listened hard but heard nothing more and so continued on their way.

The silence was broken only by the ticking of the grandmother clock. The hands on its big yellow face read 1:45.

Edward, in the lead, mimed that they should head for the back door. When they reached the scullery, he whispered, 'There's only one bolt on this door.'

Carefully, he inched it back and swung the door open.

Cool night air washed over them. Peter shivered and pulled his coat tighter around him. Together, they walked around the side of the house, pausing only when they reached the small gate. Here, Edward turned to address his companions again.

'When we get to the front gate, go through quickly and crawl along by the fence to the left, until you get to the bushes. Got it?'

'Got it,' whispered Billy.

They did as Edward had told them.

The moon was hidden behind low cloud, so the boys had to pick their way cautiously along the lane, with Edward still in the lead.

'Is it very far?' asked Peter.

'Not that far,' replied Edward. 'Why?'

'I need to go to the toilet,' Peter whispered urgently.

Edward stopped and raised his eyes to heaven. 'Well, it's either the bushes or back to the cottage!'

'Wait for me, then,' said Peter. 'I'm not going all the way back.'

He disappeared into the darkness, leaving his companions to wait for him in the middle of the dark lane.

A soft breeze made brittle leaves whisper in the tree-tops. In the distance, an owl hooted. Something scuttled through the bushes, doubtless disturbed by the boys' presence. Then, entirely without warning, the wind picked up and fallen leaves began to circle their feet with a dry, crackling sound, like skeletal fingers scratching against a coffin-lid.

'I wish Peter would hurry up,' muttered Edward.

After what seemed like forever, Peter finally reappeared. 'All done,' he said.

'Come on, then,' whispered Edward. 'Not much further now.'

He stopped when he came to a gap in the bushes that was taken up by a stile. On the far side lay a field bordered by the dark, shifting silhouettes of thin trees blown by the wind.

Peter felt the fast beating of his heart as he followed Edward and Billy over the stile. The urge to suggest that they forget about all this and go back to the warmth and safety of their beds was almost overpowering, but so was his reluctance to be branded a coward.

At last the clouds skimmed free of the moon, and all at once the field was illuminated by a sudden downpour of molten silver. And there, not more than two hundred yards away, rose the broken silhouette of the haunted abbey.

Once it must have been as big as any cathedral, but now all that remained were two long walls into which had been fashioned five high, rounded arches, and a north-facing back wall with a high, Gothic doorway. The nave roof had completely vanished, and a pile of rubble to one side marked the spot where a tower spire had once stood. Edward pointed out the remains of a postern gate and what might once have been a fountain, but overall the place had been devastated by the passage of time. Now it was a ruin, a crumbling, broken ruin. And yet in its own austere way it was beautiful.

Billy, standing beside Edward, narrowed his eyes and asked nervously, 'Where did you see the figure?'

'Over there,' Edward replied. 'Outlined in the doorway, at the top of the steps.'

The boys stared long and hard at the grey-black opening, hoping and yet dreading to see something.

'They say that it's the ghost of a monk who was caught helping smugglers hide their contraband in the abbey cellars,' Edward explained.

Peter frowned. 'I thought smugglers only operated by the sea.'

'They do. But Fenby's only a couple of miles from here. It's got a beach and everything.'

Billy was astonished. 'What? Do you mean that we're near the seaside?'

'Well, there's not much there,' said Edward, screwing up his nose. 'Just a few rocks and some sand. But it's fun to watch the fishermen when they're pulling their boats up.'

'Oh boy!' breathed Billy. 'This gets even better!'

Peter suddenly grabbed Edward's arm, almost knocking him off his feet.

'Hey!' shouted Edward. 'What...!'

He didn't get the chance to finish.

'Did ... did ... did you s-see that?' stammered Peter. 'Over there!'

He pointed to a tall lancet arch, but they could see nothing.

'What was it?' demanded Billy.

'It ... it was a man! I'm *sure* it was a man!'

'A man?' asked Edward.

'Or a *ghost?*' asked Billy.

At that moment, however, Peter was in no mood to discuss the difference. He dove for the stile, grazing his leg as he jumped down into the lane and began to run as fast as his legs would carry him back the way they'd come.

Edward tore after him with Billy in quick pursuit, Billy landing in a heap on the grassy verge before surging back up and sprinting after them.

Peter hadn't realised how fast he could run until he skidded to a halt on the gravel outside Holly Cottage. Only then did he think to look behind him, panting like an old dog on a warm day.

A few moments later Edward appeared, whispering urgently, 'Get down, Peter! Down!'

Peter threw himself to the ground as Edward, bent double, drew to a halt beside him. Then Edward started gesturing wildly with his arms to make Billy slow down before his own noisy arrival gave them away.

Billy threw himself at his friends and they all collapsed in a heap in front of the cottage gate.

'Umph!'

'Get off!'

'Sorry!'

'Look, we've got to be quiet!' Edward insisted. 'That's my mum's bedroom window up there, and if she spots us out here, we'll be in *big* trouble!'

Hearing the panic in his voice, Peter and Billy suddenly froze and held their breath.

'Right,' Edward whispered at last. 'You two follow me, and don't make a sound!'

He swung the gate open and Billy and Peter followed him across the garden, through the side gate and finally to the scullery door. Edward opened the door slowly, half-expecting to see his mother waiting for them all on the other side. But all was quiet as they tip-toed through the kitchen.

They paused for a moment at the bottom of the stairs, but the house around them remained still and silent. Matching Edward's example, they climbed each step with the most elaborate caution until they reached the top. There they stopped to listen again before finally slinking back into Edward's bedroom.

Safe at last, they quickly tore off their outer clothes to reveal the pyjamas beneath. Then Edward threw his clothes onto the chair and literally dived into bed, pulling the blankets up high.

Billy looked at his sister, content now in sleep. Then he too leapt into his bed and lay there, urging Peter to hurry.

But Peter was nothing if not a tidy boy. He wasn't content to throw his clothes *anywhere,* and he was carefully folding his jumper when he heard a noise just outside the bedroom door. He turned quickly to see Edward's mother standing in the doorway.

'Peter?' she asked curiously. 'Why on earth have you got your trousers on?'

Peter tried to form a sentence, but his mouth didn't want to cooperate. 'I … uh … I…' he began.

He looked across at Edward whose eyes were tight shut, then down at Billy who was also apparently fast asleep.

'Were you sleepwalking, dear?' asked Beryl.

Peter was tempted to say that he must have been, but said instead, 'I … er … thought I heard a noise downstairs. I … I thought it might be … you know, a burglar. But now that I think about it, I was probably just dreaming.'

It sounded pretty feeble even to his own ears, but it appeared to satisfy Edward's mother, who said, 'Well, you just hop back into bed and go back to sleep. We don't have burglars in Little Asham. There's nothing here worth stealing!'

And with that, she pulled the door shut behind her.

Billy opened one eye and peered around. 'That was close!' he breathed. 'I told you to hurry up, didn't I?'

'Oh, shut up.'

'That was pretty quick thinking, though,' admitted Edward, sitting up in bed.

But Peter took no pleasure in the compliment. 'I'm sorry I lied to your mum,' he said.

He sounded so pathetic in the darkness that Edward felt a sudden rush of sympathy for him. 'Well, it was only a *white* lie,' he replied.

Billy had started giggling. 'I wish I could've seen your face when Mrs Price came in, though! I bet it was a right picture!'

Stifling a yawn, Edward asked, 'Hey, Peter, did you *really* see a man out there?'

'I swear I did!'

'Was it a monk?' asked Billy.

'I don't know,' Peter replied honestly. 'But it certainly put the fear of God into *me!*'

Chapter Eleven

Cheeky Joe

'I can't believe that I went to bed last night and didn't bolt the back door!' said Beryl the following morning. 'That's not like me at all.'

The children were sitting at the kitchen table eating breakfast. Billy glanced at Edward, who shuffled uncomfortably as he remembered their night-time trip to the abbey. Peter looked down at his plate, a faint grin playing at his mouth.

Dismissing the matter from her mind, Beryl announced casually, 'I'm, ah, going to take a walk into the village this morning, Edward. I need some odds and ends, and Joe usually comes on a Monday, doesn't he?'

Edward stared at his mother, open-mouthed. She hadn't been into the village since–

'Edward?' she pressed.

'Uh, yes,' he replied.

Falling silent again, he toyed thoughtfully with his breakfast. Ever since his dad had died, and Mum had more or less stopped

109

going out, it had been *his* job to run all the errands. What had happened to make his mother suddenly decide to go into the village herself?

Perhaps she really *was* ill. But sneaking a look at her now, he had to admit that she certainly *looked* all right. In fact, she had seemed almost happy ever since Billy, Jeannie and Peter had come to stay. But maybe that was just a coincidence.

'You can all come with me, then,' his mother said, surprising him once again.

And to herself she added nervously, *For moral support.*

It was turning into another warm day as they walked down towards the village, but autumn was already making its presence known. Mornings were now beginning to dawn sparkly with dew, and Beryl was regularly drawn to her bedroom window by the distinctive *phee-ew* of that habitual autumn visitor, the starling. She'd also noticed increasing numbers of jays in the garden, geese flying south, wild berries appearing on bushes, and mushrooms and other fungi beginning to sprout in the moist shade beneath them.

'What's a mobile shop?' Jeannie asked suddenly.

'It's a shop on wheels that goes around the villages,' explained Edward. 'Don't you have them in London?'

'We only have shops that stand still,' said Billy. 'Lots of 'em.'

'Well, we don't have that many,' said Edward. 'That's why our one has wheels, so it can travel all over the place.'

As soon as they entered the village they spotted a large maroon-coloured Ford Model A van parked on the far side of the Green, with three women gathered around its open back doors.

Without warning, Beryl suddenly stopped in her tracks, and Edward, glancing up quickly, saw a look of uncertainty cross her face. She made a big show of muttering to herself and checking the contents of her bag, but she didn't fool him for a moment. She never had. He knew her too well for that.

She was scared.

A long, uncomfortable moment passed. Edward felt the panic in her and didn't know what to do for the best. But then, finally, she took hold of Jeannie's hand, almost as if for reassurance, and they continued on their way, albeit at a somewhat slower pace.

As they drew nearer, the children saw that the van was packed solid with every imaginable household item. An array of wooden spoons, spatulas and sieves hung from hooks on the open doors. Shelves inside the van were stacked high with cups, saucers, dishes and plates, and laid out on the floor were a selection of brooms, brushes and mops.

The proprietor was a chubby little man in his early fifties whose name was Joe Perkins. He was well-known in many a Norfolk village, where he sold his wares with a cheeky charm that brightened the day for many a lonely housewife.

One such satisfied customer, still chuckling at one of Cheeky Joe's more colourful comments, bade farewell to the two women still waiting to be served and then went on her way.

'Good morning, my love,' Joe said, addressing his next customer with an exaggerated bow. 'And what can I do you for this fine morning?'

The woman said, 'My washing line's just broken, and everything ended up in the dirt.'

'You've overloaded it, that's your trouble,' said Joe. 'Here, you'll be needin' some of this.'

And with a flourish he produced a skein of buff-coloured twine.

'Give me some of your pegs as well, while you're about it, Joe. Do you know, I've got through four sheets already, cleaning up after those filthy little vaccies.'

Beryl, standing to one side, had recognised the two women instantly. One was tall, heavy-set Norah Windom, a hard-faced woman with a spiteful twist to her near-lipless mouth. She lived by the school and her equally-surly ten year-old son, Alan, was a well-known bully. Her companion, Nell Jackson, lived in the cottage across from the old windmill just outside the village, and at the last count had seven children, all younger than Edward. She was short and slovenly in appearance, but as opinionated as Norah and very, very sure of herself.

Beryl didn't believe that she'd ever seen either woman without the other. It seemed that they could always be found gossiping together at their cottage gates or whispering conspiratorially in the village shops, and they seldom had a good word to say for anyone.

In short, they were the last people she needed to see just then.

Norah Windom glanced in Beryl's direction, registered a brief flicker of surprise and then paid for her goods. While her friend was being served, she wandered closer, and Beryl felt the woman's piggy little eyes looking her up and down as if she had no right to be there.

It was all she could do not to squirm.

'Good morning, Mrs Price,' Norah said at last. 'Not often we see you out and about.'

Beryl's throat closed tight and her heart threatened to pound itself right out of her chest. 'No, I … I haven't been well,' she managed after a moment. 'But I'm much better now.'

'Oh, good,' said Norah, her tone syrupy. 'I often see young Edward there, doing all the fetching and carrying for you. I said to my husband, that Edward Price became a man overnight after his father died. He *had* to, didn't he, the poor little tyke?'

Beryl's lips thinned. 'He's been a God-send,' she allowed.

Nell Jackson paid for her goods and joined her friend. It was only when Cheeky Joe went to serve Beryl that he finally realised who she was, and his ruddy face lit up.

'Well, who do we have here?' he asked, reaching down to take one of Beryl's hands in both of his. 'Hello, stranger! How are you, my love?'

'Hello, Joe,' Beryl replied a little shyly. 'I'm keeping fine, thank you. And yourself?'

'All the better for seein' you,' he answered with a broad, toothy smile. 'And I must say, it's a very pleasant treat indeed!'

Norah and Nell were still hovering nearby, talking to each other in hushed tones and occasionally glancing in Beryl's direction. Seeing as much, Joe lowered his voice and said, 'You think they'd have somethin' better to do with their time, wouldn't you?' Then, a bit louder, 'What can I do you for, me darlin'?'

'I need some white sewing cotton, if you've got it,' she began hesitantly. 'I'll take two reels, and some ribbon as well.'

Joe pulled out a drawer and held it up for her inspection. 'Here you go. Just help yourself.'

While Beryl made her choice, Joe pulled faces at the children, then hopped out of the van to play-fight them on the grass until they were all hanging off his arms, laughing.

'All right!' he moaned at last, 'you win! But only 'cause I'm not as young as I used to be, and you've got me outnumbered!'

Straightening again, he observed, 'Looks like you got three nice ones there, Mrs Price. All from London, I take it?'

'Yes, all from London. And they're no trouble, so I can hardly complain.'

'I dunno, though,' he sighed, climbing slowly back into the van. 'What do you make of all this war lark, eh?'

Before she could form a reply, Norah Windom spoke up. 'My husband said that if Chamberlain had fought in the last lot instead of sittin' on his backside in Whitehall, he wouldn't have been in such a hurry to declare war *this* time.'

'He's got a point,' allowed Joe, who had seen action himself at Mons, Ypres, the Somme and Shaiba. 'But when all's said and done, *someone* has to make a stand against the bully-boys. Just look what they did on

Saturday – torpedoed a civilian ship off the coast of Ireland an' killed more than a hundred people! Anyway, it's not as if we're on our own. New Zealand declared war this mornin'.'

'Ay,' said Nell Jackson. 'But the Danes and the Irish say they want to keep out of it.'

'I think they've got the right idea,' Beryl said impulsively.

That earned her a glare from Norah and Nell, who clearly felt that she had committed a crime by daring to voice an opinion. She flushed at becoming the centre of attention and felt, foolishly, that she needed to justify herself.

'I mean,' she flustered, 'if we *all* kept out of it, there'd be no-one to fight the war in the first place.'

There followed a moment of heavy silence until Joe said, '*Exactly,* my love. Now, what else would you like?'

Beryl wanted a number of things, but most of all just then she wanted to go home and *sit* down before she *fell* down. Her heart was rushing again and she felt a little faint. It was nerves, that was all, and she *knew* it was nerves, but somehow that didn't help. It only made things worse.

'There *was* something else,' she said breathlessly, playing for time, 'but I … I can't, ah, for the life of me think what it was now.'

She gathered up her wares and made to pay for them, but Joe caught her hand in his and said softly, 'You're shaking like a leaf, Mrs Price! Are you all right?'

Beryl nodded. 'I'm fine. It's just ... well, I haven't been out in a while. I suppose I've grown a bit too used to my own company.'

He nodded. 'Well, suppose I lock up and see you home safely?'

'I wouldn't hear of it.'

'It's no trouble, honest.'

'No, I ... I'm fine. *Really.* But I do appreciate it, Joe.'

He frowned. 'Well, if you're sure...'

Beryl nodded. She'd gone as pale as chalk. 'Thanks anyway. Hopefully I'll, ah, see you again next week.'

'There'll be an argument if I don't see *you,*' he returned. Then, catching her eye, he added quietly, 'Slow and steady wins the race, love.'

As they started back towards home and left Norah and Nell behind them, Beryl felt some of the panic subsiding at last. She still felt sweaty and shaky, but more than that she actually began to feel proud of herself. She'd *done* it. And though it had been terrifying, it hadn't been anywhere near as terrifying as she'd expected it to be. In fact, a part of her was already looking forward to the next time.

Edward, still concerned about her, followed the others across the Green towards the church. Billy dropped back to join him and whispered, 'Do you think we can go back to the abbey today?'

'We might be able to,' Edward replied distractedly. 'I'll ask Mum.'

Grateful for the opportunity to engage her in conversation, he hurried up to Beryl and asked. She considered the idea for a moment, then said, 'Well, I suppose so. But don't go taking liberties, Edward. You know Mr Palmer doesn't take kindly to trespassers!'

This was a reference to the previous summer, when Edward, on his way to Fenby, had made the mistake of taking a short-cut across Mr Palmer's field. The farmer had chased after him, ranting and raving, and it was only by luck that Edward had been able to outdistance him. Unfortunately for the boy, however, Mr Palmer had recognised him, and later paid Beryl a very unpleasant visit, during which he told her to keep her son under control, or else.

Even to this day, Edward didn't like to think what *or else* meant, so he made sure he kept to the lane whenever he had reason to go to Fenby, and always walked a little quicker when he passed the Palmer cottage.

When they got home, the children helped themselves to an apple each from the orchard, then set off in the direction of the abbey.

The boys made no direct mention of the previous night's adventure, lest Jeannie accidentally gave the game away, but they could hardly wait to return to the site and have a closer look around.

'I'd hate to come here after dark,' said Billy, throwing a loaded glance at Peter.

Peter kicked at a large stone. 'Oh, I don't know,' he replied. 'I quite like a midnight stroll every now and then!'

'Anyone would think that you two had been here before!' chuckled Edward.

Jeannie wandered along beside the boys, completely unaware of their secret. She had been polishing her apple against the material of one of her new dresses ever since they left the orchard behind them, and now finally took a bite.

'*Ow!*' she wailed. 'My tooth! Look!'

As the boys crowded around her, she curled back her top lip to reveal a gap where her tooth had been just seconds before.

'Where is it, then?' asked Billy. 'Don't swallow it, whatever you do!'

Peter took hold of Jeannie's hand, complete with apple. 'Here it is!' he exclaimed, holding her hand high. 'It's still stuck in the apple!'

'Yuk!' cried Edward. 'You'd better put it somewhere safe.'

'What, the apple?' asked Billy.

'The *tooth,*' said Edward. 'It's worth

money to the Tooth Fairy.'

Jeannie frowned up at him. 'What's that?' she asked.

'Haven't you ever heard of the Tooth Fairy?'

'No.'

'She's the one who leaves you threepence if you put the tooth under your pillow.'

Jeannie's eyes went round. '*Really?*' she asked.

'Really,' confirmed Edward. 'But you'd better tell my mum first, so that she can let the Chief Fairy know.'

Jeannie took the tooth and carefully put it in the pocket of her dress.

A few moments later they reached the stile and the boys climbed onto the top-most step. Billy reached down to Jeannie and said, 'Here, give me your hand.'

With the sun out and a gentle breeze blowing, the abbey looked considerably more inviting by day than it had by night. The crumbling walls were awash with ragwort, its bright yellow flowers appearing to dance in the breeze.

They all jumped down into the field and made their way through the tall grass until they stood in front of the tall doorway. The wide steps were cracked and moss-covered, and what had once been a flat, tiled floor was now little more than a carpet of grass stippled with daisies.

Billy sprinted to an opening on the right, where an arch had once stood, then scaled the mound of rubble that was all that remained of the tower spire. There, he sat down and ate his apple while the others caught up. A herd of cows occupied the field beyond the abbey, and a collection of farm buildings could just be seen in the distance.

Edward joined Billy on the rocky pinnacle. 'On a fine day you can see the sea from here,' he said, pointing in an easterly direction. 'Just beyond those trees over there.'

Billy looked in the direction that Edward had indicated, where on the horizon a deeper shade of blue stood out between land and sky. He was mesmerized by the wide open space. 'There's a lot of sky here,' he muttered.

Peter and Jeannie climbed up next to the two boys and stretched out in the sun. They stayed like that for a long time, neither talking nor moving. The silence and stillness was comfortable, and the abbey itself felt like a home from home.

Chapter Twelve

Billy vs Bully

A few days later Peter received his first letter from home. The postman called early and Beryl gathered the mail from the mat as the children sat down to breakfast. There was a letter from her sister in Devon, some official-looking papers regarding her three evacuees and a small white envelope addressed to *Master Peter Murray*.

Beryl returned into the kitchen. 'Peter, you have a letter,' she announced. The look of disappointment on Billy's face didn't go unnoticed. 'I expect you two will have a letter from mummy tomorrow,' she added, placing a hand on Billy's shoulder. 'Your mum has probably been busy.'

Peter, meanwhile, had torn open the envelope and now read:

Dear Peter,
I was glad to hear that the three of you arrived safely and are in good hands. I hope you are all behaving yourselves.
You wouldn't recognise our back garden now, as we have an Anderson shelter at the bottom.

Thelma and Kit helped me to put it together, so now I have somewhere to go if there's an air-raid. I might even try growing some flowers and vegetables outside. The first night that you were away was also the start of the Blackout, so like you in the country we no longer have any street-lamps and have had to put our thick winter curtains up early so that no light shows from outside.

I have heard from Daddy and he says to send his love, as you know I send mine.

I will be coming up to see you very soon, with extra clothes and perhaps even a surprise or two. Until then, be a good boy and help Mrs Price all you can.

Lots of love,
MUMMY
xxxxxx

Peter folded the letter and slipped it into his pocket, a contented smile playing at his lips.

'Is mummy well, Peter?' asked Beryl.

'Yes. She says that she might be coming to see me soon!'

'I wish that Mummy had written to *us,*' whined Jeannie, looking a little down in the mouth.

Billy only scowled.

'She will,' Beryl said with a little more conviction than she actually felt. 'You just wait and see. Give it a day or two. After all, you haven't even been here a *week* yet.'

She cleared the table, then picked up a small package from the dresser. 'Edward, be a love and pop this up to the lady staying with Gran. Her name's Mary. Tell her it's a little something for Patsy.'

She hadn't ventured out again since the visit to Joe's mobile shop, but had spent her free time making a dress for Mary's little girl.

'Oh, and tell Gran I'll pop up to see her soon for a chat,' she added.

The walk into the village was a solemn affair. Billy wasn't very talkative and Jeannie kept dragging her heels. Peter, though delighted with his letter from home, had now fallen silent as he tried to work out just what those surprises his mother had mentioned might be.

'Have you lot got cloth ears or something?' Edward asked suddenly.

'Eh?'

'What was that?'

'I just asked you if you fancied going back to the abbey later,' Edward explained.

Billy shrugged. 'If you like,' he mumbled, his hands wedged firmly into the pockets of his shorts.

'What's the matter, Billy?' Peter asked, noting Billy's lack of enthusiasm.

'Nothin',' growled Billy.

How *could* he tell Peter what was bothering him? Peter would only think he was jealous, and the worst of it was that he *was* jealous. Why couldn't he and Jeannie have had a letter from *their* mum? Why couldn't he have a daddy to send him *his* love? Blimey, he didn't even *know* his dad!

Although he almost hated to admit it, he liked being here with Peter and Edward, enjoying the freedom and all that wide open countryside. Jeannie was enjoying it, too. So why did he miss the slum they called home so much? All he'd ever known there were bare walls and empty cupboards, of being left alone with Jeannie and feeling the heavy weight of responsibility for his own upbringing as well as hers.

He felt confused. Why couldn't his mum be normal, like Mrs Price? For one fleeting moment he felt that he didn't ever want to go back home, that he wanted to stay here forever, and that made him feel even more rotten, almost disloyal.

As they approached the end of the lane, they saw two boys slouching towards them from the opposite direction, kicking at tufts of grass as they came. Edward recognised them both. They were in his class at school, although both were about a year older than he. The tallest was Alan Windom, Norah Windom's bully of a son. The other, a skinny, runny-nosed lad by the name of Lenny Cornford, came from a farm just outside the village. When they recognised Edward they pulled up sharp, and Alan deliberately raised his voice.

'Look at those vaccies,' he said to his companion, bending to pick up a stone. His voice heavy with contempt, he added, 'They act like they own the village.'

Billy, still in a world of his own, had paused to wait for Jeannie, who was still dawdling behind. When the stone buzzed past his head, he flinched.

'Oi! Watch it!'

Alan puffed himself up. He was heavy-set, like his mother, with full cheeks and dark, deep-set eyes, and dark hair that hung limply across his forehead.

'Don't you tell *me* what to do in my own village, squirt!' he returned. He stalked towards Billy, fists clenched, but Billy, determined that the older boy wouldn't get the better of him, stood his ground.

'Come on, Billy,' Edward called worriedly. 'Don't take any notice of him. Let's just go back.'

Alan pulled a face. 'Yeah, that's it, *Billy-Goat*. Go back where you came from!'

Already in a foul temper, Billy was in no mood to suffer fools gladly. He took a step toward Alan but Edward quickly stepped in and grabbed his arm.

'Come on,' he urged again.

Before he could say more, Alan grabbed

the package he'd been carrying. 'What do we have here, then?' he asked, and threw it to Lenny.

It landed in the dirt at Lenny's feet, and Billy made a quick dive for it. But blond, hawk-faced Lenny quickly snatched it up, and with a giggle threw it back to Alan.

'Give it here!' called Edward.

'What's it worth?' grinned Alan. Without waiting for a reply, he tossed the package high into the air. It flew in an arc and vanished into the bushes by the side of the road.

'You idiot!' grated Edward.

Alan looked as if he'd just been slapped. '*What* did you call me?'

Billy could see the fire in Alan's eyes and knew that Edward was within a cat's whisker of taking a punch on the nose. Quickly, he threw himself at the bully, his momentum carrying them both to the ground.

They tumbled over in a tangle, each trying to get the better of the other, and though Billy put up a game struggle, Alan was older and heavier, and soon had him pinned to the ground.

'*Len!*' he roared.

Lenny, looking thin-legged in his grubby grey shorts, immediately came running to give him a hand, but before he could reach the combatants, a furious yell stopped them all in their tracks. A moment later Maude Coker, the Land Army girl, brought her bicycle to a sharp halt and rung her bell furiously to make them break it up.

She dismounted and hurried over to the tangled boys, towering over Alan as she grabbed him by the arms and dragged him away from Billy. 'Just what do you think you're doing?' she demanded. 'Acting the bully again, I suppose! I've a mind to tell your mother about you!'

'Do what you like,' muttered Alan.

'What was that?'

'Nothing.'

Billy got to his feet, brushing dirt off of his clothes.

'Are you all right, Billy-boy?' Maude asked with concern.

'I'm all right,' Billy replied, adding disdainfully, 'He fights like a girl.'

Alan went to hit him again but thought better of it when Maude snapped, 'Don't you dare!'

Peter, meanwhile, had wandered off into the bushes to retrieve the package, while Jeannie stood beside Edward, frightened by what had just happened.

'I've got it,' yelled Peter from the other side of the lane. A moment later he reappeared, holding up the package. 'The paper's a bit torn,' he added.

Alan and Lenny now stood meekly to one

side, Lenny in particular giving the impression that butter would have a very hard time melting in his mouth.

'I hope for your sakes that you haven't ruined whatever was in there!' Maude snapped sternly. 'Go on, off with you!'

Lenny immediately started walking away, but Alan felt obliged to give the children one last glare before he made his own exit.

'I think it's all right,' Peter said at last, handing the package back to Edward.

Jeannie came up to Maude and took hold of her hand. She offered the Land Army girl a tremulous smile.

'Where's your tooth gone, little 'un?' Maude asked in mock surprise.

'It fell out!' said Jeannie, continuing excitedly, 'I told Mrs Price, an' she told the Chief Fairy, an' then the Chief Fairy told the Tooth Fairy, an' the Tooth Fairy gave me threepence for it while I was asleep!'

'Threepence, eh?' said Maude. 'I *am* impressed. When I was your age, I was lucky if the Tooth Fairy gave me a ha'penny!' She looked at the quartet. 'Where are you off to, anyway?'

'We're delivering this to the lady staying at Gran's,' said Edward.

'Come on, then,' said Maude, picking up her bicycle. 'I'm going your way.'

Gran's front door was standing ajar as they walked up the short path a few minutes later, and they could hear voices coming from within. Edward knocked loudly.

'Hello, who is it?' called Gran. A moment later she appeared in the hallway, carrying a tray laden with sandwiches. 'Oh, it's Edward and his friends,' she said. 'Come in, the lot of you.'

The four children went inside and followed Gran into a tiny, sun-filled sitting room, where three young women were laughing and chatting, one of them bouncing a baby boy on her knee.

The children stood shyly to one side while Gran set the tray down on a long table in the centre of the room. Then Gran said, 'What can I do for you, Edward?'

'Uh, Mum sent this package for Mary,' Edward replied.

'For *me?*' asked a voice from the corner.

Edward walked over to the woman who was bouncing the baby on her knee. The baby immediately reached for the package and began to guide it toward his mouth.

'No, Frankie, you'll make it all wet!' Mary said with a chuckle. 'Here, Cis, take him a minute, would you?' she handed the infant to the woman sitting next to her and said, 'These are my sisters, Cis and Lil. They've come up from London to see us.'

Hearing the name, Billy said, '*We* come from London as well!'

'Do you, love?' asked Cis. 'Which part?'

'Bethnal Green,' Billy said proudly.

'What about you?' Cis asked Peter, who was standing quietly behind Jeannie.

'I'm from Bethnal Green, too.'

'Well, we come from Stoke Newington. That's not far from where you live. Us Londoners, we've got to stick together! Isn't that right, love?'

She winked at Peter, who grinned.

During the exchange, Mary had opened the package and pulled out the tiny dress it contained. It was a replica of the one that Jeannie was wearing, cut from a pale green floral material with tiny puffed sleeves that were edged with delicate white lace.

Mary said, 'Oh, Lil, Cis, look at this!'

There was a round of appreciative *oohs* and *aahs* as Mary held the garment up for everyone to see, and Edward felt a swell of pride for his mother.

'It's like mine!' yelled Jeannie, stepping forward and holding her own dress out in front of her.

Mary's other sister, Lil, reached out to take Jeannie by the hand. 'And don't you look the pretty one wearing it!' she complimented.

'Oh, you must thank mummy for me,' Mary said to Edward. 'I'll pop down to see her again to thank her myself. Would you tell her that?'

Edward nodded.

'Will you children stay for some tea and cake?' asked Gran.

The offer was tempting, but so was the prospect of spending the afternoon at the abbey. 'No thanks, Gran,' said Edward, glancing at the others. 'We'd better be getting back.'

They said their goodbyes and left.

Chapter Thirteen

Adrift

Maude felt a vague stab of unease when she spotted Police Constable Salmon cycling through the streets of Little Asham that Friday afternoon.

It had been a relatively quiet week. South Africa had declared war on Germany on 6th September. Canada was expected to follow suit in a matter of days. Japan and the United States had both proclaimed their neutrality, and there'd been rumours that the RAF had recently clashed with the German navy in the North Sea. But aside from this, the war hadn't really affected anyone much, and Maude couldn't help thinking the last six days had been a sort of honeymoon period: the calm, if you like, before the storm.

PC Salmon, a skinny young man with an eager, helpful manner, had cycled all the away from Fenby. He now made directly for the church, where he held a hurried conversation with the vicar, Mr Farrow. Shortly thereafter, PC Salmon remounted his bike and headed back to Fenby. The vicar walked slowly up the lane toward Holly Cottage.

Beryl was baking bread, and the children were in the orchard, picking blackberries, when there came a soft knock at the front door. She wiped her hands on a tea-towel and went to answer it, fully expecting to see Mary Roberts on the step. To her surprise, however, she found the vicar instead.

'Mrs Price,' said Mr Farrow. 'I wonder if I might come in for a moment?'

Puzzled, Beryl nevertheless opened the door wide. 'Yes, of course. Is everything–?'

'Are the children around?' interrupted the vicar. He looked very serious, shocked almost, and certainly troubled.

'They're in the orchard.'

'Ah,' he said. 'Good.'

He went through to the parlour, a tall, thin man of about forty-five, pale-skinned, bespectacled and balding prematurely. When Beryl entered the room and closed the door behind her, he said, 'I'm afraid I have some rather bad news.'

Beryl froze. Her throat closed, her breathing turned shallow, and she heard herself say, 'What is it? What's happened?'

'It's Mrs Curtis,' said the vicar, his voice still low. 'Billy and Jeannie's mother.'

'Yes?'

'There's been an accident,' said the vicar. He took off his round, dark-framed glasses and gave them a quick, nervous polish. 'I'm afraid she's dead.'

Billy looked down at his hands, which were dyed purple with the juice of the black-berries they'd been picking, and said, 'I don't think I can fit any more into this basin.'

Edward and Peter had moved a little further along the hedge to a spot where the fruit grew thicker.

'Do you think this'll be enough?' called Billy.

Turning his head to reply, Edward noticed his mother and Mr Farrow coming towards them from the direction of the cottage, carefully picking their way through the long grass. Peter spotted them too, and murmured in surprise, 'It's the vicar. I wonder what *he* wants?'

Edward turned and smiled at the new-comer, but received no response. Actually, Mr Farrow looked rather grim, and Edward wondered if he'd seen them misbehaving in church the previous Sunday and come to scold them.

But then the vicar said, 'Good morning,

children. I see you've all been busy.'

He looked around for Jeannie and spotted her a few yards away, trying to untangle her dress from a stubborn bramble.

'Here, let me help,' he called, and went over to her. 'There, that's it, all free again!'

He took the child by the hand and led her back to the others. Then he said, 'I'd like to have a little chat with you and your brother, if I may.'

Billy frowned at him. Edward and Peter exchanged a glance.

'Boys,' said Beryl, addressing them in a near whisper. 'Come with me.'

Edward said, 'What–?'

'Just come with me.'

Edward saw then that his mother had tears in her eyes, and wordlessly they both did as she said.

As they walked away, Mr Farrow knelt before Billy and Jeannie. The afternoon was warm and bright, and a gentle breeze filtered through the trees, making their branches sway and creak. He said, 'I'm afraid I have some rather bad news for you, children.'

Something changed in Billy's eyes. They suddenly became unreadable.

'It's your mummy,' said Mr Farrow. 'She had an accident last night. I'm sorry to say–'

'She's dead, isn't she?' said Billy.

The vicar looked him directly in the face. 'Yes, Billy,' he said gently. 'I'm afraid she is.'

Billy looked down at the grass at his feet. After a moment he asked without looking up, 'Was it the Germans?'

Mr Farrow smiled sadly. 'No. No, it wasn't the Germans. It was just an accident.'

For a moment he debated going into further detail. But where was the point? He'd just delivered the worst news these children were every likely to receive. Did he have to make the deed even more distasteful by telling them how needless their mother's death had been?

As he understood it from PC Salmon, the woman and her common-law husband, a man called George Hesketh, had spent the previous evening drinking at a number of local pubs. They were making their way home through the Blackout when an argument erupted between them. One thing led to another, there was a scuffle and they traded blows, with Mrs Curtis receiving a bloody nose in the fray. She had stormed off in a rage, and ten minutes later was hit by a van as she crossed a main road close to her home. The police said she had been so drunk that in all likelihood she neither saw nor heard the van until it struck her.

Did these children need to hear that? Of course not. But what *did* they need to hear? A verse from Romans came to mind. *And we know that all things work together for good to them that love God, to them who are called according to His purpose.* But what could that possibly mean to children so young?

At last Billy looked up, looked him right in the eye, and Mr Farrow almost recoiled from the turmoil of anger and sorrow and resignation he saw in the boy's hazel gaze.

'She's gone, then,' Billy said flatly. He'd always known it would happen one day. It had been his biggest fear for as long as he could remember. 'She won't be coming back.'

It wasn't a question.

Mr Farrow licked his lips and said, 'Billy. Do you know where your father is?'

Billy thought for a moment. No-one had ever asked him that before. 'He went away when I was little and Jeannie was a baby,' he mumbled. 'Mummy says … said … he didn't want to be with us anymore.'

'Oh, I'm sure that's not true.'

'Why did she say it, then?'

The vicar had no answer for that. 'Do you have any aunts and uncles?'

'Only Uncle George.'

'Grandparents?'

'No-one,' said Billy.

'Well,' sighed the vicar, 'don't worry about anything. Everything will be all right.'

'How?' asked Billy.

Mr Farrow shook his head and shrugged. 'The authorities will take care of you,' he replied. 'But in the meantime, you have to be strong, Billy. Your sister's relying on you to look after her.'

Billy looked at him through suddenly-old eyes and said coldly, 'I've *always* looked after her.'

Beryl said goodbye to Mr Farrow, closed the front door after him, took a deep breath and then returned to the kitchen, where she found Billy and Jeannie sitting at the table, exactly where she'd just left them.

She could only imagine what was going through their little minds now, and wasn't entirely sure what to do to soften what had been a dreadful blow. But she had to do *something*, as much for her own sake as theirs, so she took a jug of milk from the larder and filled two glasses, which she then placed in front of them.

Jeannie took a swallow of milk and wiped one hand across her chin. 'I'm hungry,' she said.

Beryl gave her a shaky smile. She was still so young that she didn't properly understand what had just happened, and it broke her heart to see it. She took a large tin down from the dresser and popped some biscuits onto a plate.

'Now *listen*,' she said firmly. 'You're not to worry about *anything*, do you understand me? We'll work something out.'

The two children sat looking up at her.

'We're all alone now, though, ain't we?' said Billy. 'Got no mum, got no dad, got nowhere to live, nowhere to go.'

The last thing he wanted to do then or ever was cry. But as the news finally began to sink in, he couldn't help himself. He bowed his head, his eyes screwed shut, his lips twisted and all at once a sob that was pure anguish escaped from him, after which his shoulders began to heave.

Beryl hurried around the table, knelt beside him, held him tight while he broke his little heart.

'You just let it all out,' she whispered, choking up herself. 'It'll make you feel better, believe me.'

Jeannie, still not fully understanding this new turn of events, slipped off her chair and stood beside them, her own bottom lip starting to quiver. Beryl snaked an arm around her and drew her close, and they stayed like that for what seemed like a very long time.

Chapter Fourteen

The Photograph

While the vicar had been speaking to Billy and Jeannie, Beryl had taken Edward and Peter into the parlour and told them what had happened. It was, of course, the very last thing the boys had been expecting.

'Will they have to go away?' Edward had asked worriedly.

'I don't know yet,' she replied. 'We'll just have to wait and see. But I think we all need to carry on as normal, for their sakes.'

'I hope *my* mum will be all right,' muttered Peter.

'Of course she will, Peter. You mustn't start worrying about her. She'll be coming up to see you soon, won't she?'

The lad seemed to brighten at the prospect.

'Do you think they might want to go out and play?' asked Edward.

'Well, you can always ask.'

'They might like to go down to the abbey,' suggested Peter. He thought that it might do them good to spend some time at what they now considered to be their special place.

When they entered the kitchen sometime later, the boys were surprised to see that Billy looked more or less like his usual self. They could see that he'd been crying, but passed no comment. He looked up from his milk and offered them a faint smile, but said he didn't care whether he went to the abbey or not.

They went, anyway.

For the rest of that afternoon, Edward and Peter tried to engage their friends in just about anything and everything they could think of. For her part, Jeannie seemed content just to stay close to her brother, but in truth there was really no way of telling what was going through her mind just then.

They sat on the fallen tower beside the abbey ruins, basking in the late afternoon sunshine. Billy couldn't think of anything to say, and wasn't in much of a mood for conversation, anyway. Though he'd been reluctant to come, however, he was glad that he'd allowed the others to drag him along after all. He'd grown to love this spot, with its panoramic views of the cattle-dotted fields and the sea beyond, the scent of wild grasses and the raucous sound of birds circling high above. It was a world away from everything he'd known in London.

On their previous visit, Edward had claimed a fallen slab of masonry that was shaped roughly like a throne, complete with moss-covered back-rest. Now he sat there with his hands behind his head and said, 'I wish we didn't have to go to school on Monday.'

Peter, who had been sprawled out on a ledge nearby, sat up quickly, shielding his gentle blue eyes from the sun. 'Do you suppose we'll be in the same class?' he asked. 'We're almost the same age, after all.'

'I don't think we have enough desks,' said Edward.

Jeannie looked up from where she was sitting cross-legged in the grass, searching for a four-leaf clover amid the mass of cone-shaped flower-heads that surrounded her. 'Do you think I'll be in your class, too?' she asked, looking from one boy to the other. 'I don't want to be in a class on my own.'

'We might not be here for much longer, anyway,' Billy reminded her moodily, hugging his knees to his chin.

'I don't want to go away again,' fretted Jeannie.

'My mum says that everything will carry on as it is,' Edward offered.

'I hope so,' admitted Billy. 'I mean, I like living in your house.'

'So do I,' said Jeannie, also addressing Edward. 'That way, *your* mum can be *our* mum as well.'

The weekend came and went, and almost

before they knew it, Monday – the first day of the new school year – dawned sharp and misty.

Billy and Jeannie had coped well in the preceding days, and Beryl had made a point of encouraging them in everything they did. At first, however, she'd debated the wisdom of sending them off to school. After all, Billy still wasn't right – he was too quiet, too jaded, and understandably down in the dumps. But it was probably best if they carried on as normal.

So it was that all three boys came down to breakfast that morning wearing grey flannel shorts and clean white shirts, with Jeannie dressed in a pale grey pinafore Beryl had made for her over the weekend.

After breakfast, she led the children down the lane towards the school. As they approached the Green, the sound of a hand-bell carried to them on the breeze, loud, then soft, loud, then soft. The school gate was now open, and pupils old and new were descending upon it from all directions, with parents or guardians in tow.

All at once, however, a shrill, prolonged whistle cut through the air, and they suddenly became aware of a disturbance in the crowd off to their right. A short, portly man wearing a coarse brown jacket and a black tin helmet was shoving urgently through the throng. In his mid-fifties, he huffed and puffed with every hurried step, occasionally blowing a whistle to clear the way ahead, until at last he came face to face with the neat-looking young woman who was ringing the bell.

'Hey, you there!' yelled the man in the tin hat. 'Miss Matthews! You can't do that! Don't you know there's a war on?'

The bell-ringer, Miss Matthews, immediately stopped. She was in her early twenties, pale-skinned and fair-haired, and she wore a mustard-coloured top over a loose brown skirt. She blushed furiously as she said, 'What? *Really*, Mr King–'

'It mustn't happen again!' the portly man interrupted, his tone firm. 'A hand-rung bell means there's poison gas around!' He drew himself up to his full height, which of course didn't take him terribly long. 'It says so in my handbook!'

All at once he seemed to grow aware of his audience, and positively basked in the attention. Reaching up, he tapped meaningfully at his tin hat. It was black, with a white *W* painted on the front. 'As your ARP warden,' he explained haughtily, 'it's *my* duty to ring any bells.'

A tall, severe-looking lady a couple of years younger than the warden suddenly appeared in the gateway, doubtless drawn by all the commotion. She gazed down at the little man as she had probably gazed down upon many a naughty schoolboy in the past. It was an unnerving experience, even for those watching, and the warden took an involuntary pace backwards.

'That's Mrs Abbott,' Edward whispered excitedly to the others. 'She's my teacher. Yours too, probably.'

Peter hoped not. She was an imposing, full-bodied woman wearing a double-breasted navy-blue dress with a cream-coloured collar and matching cuffs. Her hair was black shot through with a dusting of grey, and she wore it swept back from a well-defined face with a dark complexion and high cheekbones. Her dark, glittering eyes surveyed the warden through oval, wire-framed spectacles.

'Is there a problem here, Mr King?' she demanded authoritatively.

Again Mr King touched his fingers to the rim of his tin hat, but this time as a gesture of respect. 'Unauthorised use of a hand-bell,' he explained importantly. 'It says in my handbook that a hand-bell may only be rung in the event of a–'

'–of a poison gas attack,' finished Mrs Abbott. 'Yes, I heard you the first time. I imagine *everybody* did. But how, pray, were we to *know* that? Surely, as the warden responsible for our Air Raid Precautions, it was your duty to come and tell us.'

'I did,' said the warden. But he added in a less confident tone, 'Didn't I?'

'No, Mr King,' said Mrs Abbott. 'You did *not.*'

Glancing down at the tips of his boots, the warden muttered, 'I been so busy with my new duties, I must have neglected to let you know.'

'Well, we shan't ring the bell again,' said Mrs Abbott.

'Thank you, ma'am.'

'You are entirely welcome,' said Mrs Abbott. 'But, Mr King...'

'Yes, ma'am?'

'If you ever address Miss Matthews in that tone of voice again, I will have you stripped of your title and see to it that someone less *abrasive* and more *efficient* is appointed in your place.'

Mr King stiffened. Some of the nearest onlookers drew breath at the threat. But after a moment the warden deflated and said softly, 'I don't believe you'll find that necessary, ma'am.'

And with that he turned and shoved irritably back through the crowd.

'Wow,' muttered Peter. 'What a dragon!'

'Peter!'

'Sorry, Mrs Price.'

They said their goodbyes to Beryl and then the four children went through the gate and into the building itself, with Jeannie clinging to Billy for dear life.

The school was tiny, just a foyer, two

classrooms and a small office where Mrs Abbot saw to all the administration. Edward had said that there were eight children in his class and another five in what he called the baby class. Since around fifty evacuees had been taken into Little Asham, Peter wondered how on earth Mrs Abbott was going to fit everyone in.

Mrs Abbott and her colleague, Miss Matthews, ushered the children into the largest of the two classrooms and told them to stand around the edge of the room.

The centre was occupied by a handful of wooden desks and chairs. A tall blackboard on an easel stood down at the far end, beside a highly-polished desk.

Behind the desk stood a third woman. Slight of build beneath her cotton summer dress, she had short black hair and warm brown eyes. Spotting her, Peter immediately jabbed Billy in the ribs.

'Oi, watch it!'

'That woman!' hissed Peter. 'She's the one who looked after us on the train!'

Billy studied her more closely. Peter was right. He remembered that she'd told him he was quite an artist.

Mrs Abbott stood in front of the blackboard and clapped her hands sharply to get their attention.

'Quiet!' she snapped, and silence immediately filled the room. 'I want to see everyone facing front! That's it! Nice straight backs, and arms at your sides!'

There was a slight shuffling of feet as the children did as they were told.

Mrs Abbott introduced herself for the benefit of the newcomers and told them that she was the headmistress of Little Asham School.

'I want the children in my class to sit down at their desks,' she instructed.

She then waited while the children, including Edward, Alan Windom and Lenny Cornford, all took their places, Alan throwing Billy a murderous glance as he did so.

'Now,' she continued, 'I would like Miss Matthews' class to line up at the front.'

The five smaller children did as they were told.

That just left the evacuees.

'The rest of you,' said Mrs Abbott, picking up a school register which had been sitting on the desk, 'are new to both the village and this school. However, I do not expect that it will take you very long to settle in. We will do our best to make your stay here a pleasant and informative one. All I ask in return is that you behave yourselves, show respect for your elders and work hard. Now … when I call out your names, you will come to the front of the class and join Miss Matthews' group.'

She began to read from the register, and

the younger evacuees dutifully joined the group – all, that was, except Jeannie. When her name was called, she clung even tighter to Billy's hand, clearly reluctant to be parted from him.

'*You*, girl,' called Mrs Abbott, peering at Jeannie over the rims of her glasses. 'Is your name Jean Curtis?'

'Jeannie,' Jeannie corrected quietly.

'Well, you must come when your name is called.'

'I don't want to.'

'You don't really have a *choice*,' said Mrs Abbott sternly. 'Now, come along!'

Jeannie looked up at Billy, her eyes filling with tears. 'I don't have to go, do I, Billy?'

Billy glared at Mrs Abbott and said, 'Can't she stay with me? She's only little.'

Mrs Abbott's lips thinned. 'No, she can-*not*.'

Billy drew a breath, softening his gaze when he looked back at his sister. 'You'd better go, then, I suppose. Go on, it'll be all right, just like school back home.'

She didn't look thoroughly convinced.

'I'll see you at playtime,' he muttered to encourage her.

Reluctantly, Jeannie let go of his hand and went to join the others.

At length Miss Matthews led her group out to the other classroom. Watching them leave, Peter heaved a sigh of relief. At least he, Billy and Edward were still together!

'The following children will now line up at the front!' snapped Mrs Abbott.

She called a further thirty names from her register. Billy's was one of them, but Peter's wasn't.

'You are now under the care and tutelage of Miss Ferguson, here,' said Mrs Abbott, glancing at the teacher who had shared the journey from London with them. 'The rest of you will stay in *this* class.'

Peter looked at Billy, 'Bad luck,' he whispered.

Billy shrugged.

Miss Ferguson led Billy's group back out into the morning sunshine. Looking around, Billy wondered where they were going. There were no classrooms out here, just a big, freshly-mown field bordered by hedges and trees.

The teacher led them around to a small, paved area to one side of the school. Here there stood a blackboard and an old ladderback chair.

'Sit down, children!' called Miss Ferguson.

They sat in a semi-circle in front of the blackboard. The teacher studied them for a moment, then smiled to set them all at ease. She had prominent cheekbones, a very well-defined jaw and a cleft chin. 'Well,' she said. 'What do you think of our new classroom?'

Some of the children giggled, but Billy wasn't one of them.

'As you heard just now,' the teacher continued, 'my name is Miss Ferguson.'

She turned to the blackboard and spelled it out in large, even letters.

'Like you, I suppose I am a sort of evacuee,' she continued. 'I taught at a school in North London, until all of my children were sent to the country. I decided to come along as well, so that I might continue to teach, albeit in a much different environment.

'So, there we have it. You know *my* name. Now I want to know *yours.*'

Billy sighed. He had a feeling it was going to be a very long day.

When they got home that afternoon, Beryl told them that a Child Welfare officer called Mrs Pritchard had called in their absence. She would be taking Billy and Jeannie to London on Friday to attend their mother's funeral.

Billy had never been to a funeral before, and was more than a little disturbed by the news. 'Do we *have* to go?' he asked.

'Well, it's only right that you do, Billy,' Beryl replied gently. 'And it's nothing to be afraid of. You'll be back here again before you know it.'

But she didn't know that for sure. The fate

151

of the children had still to be decided. She felt that she had to give the boy *something* to look forward to, though.

'What do they do at a funeral? asked Jeannie, who was as wary about it as her brother.

Beryl didn't even have to think about her reply. She'd had this same conversation once before, with Edward, after Jack had died.

'Well, it's just a chance for you to remember all the things you loved about your mother before she goes off to Heaven,' she explained.

'An' then we can come home again,' Billy pressed.

He'd used the word *home* without even thinking about it.

'Well, not right away,' she replied.

'What?'

'Mrs Prtichard will collect you on Friday morning and take you back to London. The funeral's at two o'clock. After that, you'll stay the night with a woman called Mrs Brown – she acts as a foster mother for the local authority – and then Mrs Pritchard will fetch you back here on Saturday morning.'

Billy didn't like it, but he supposed it could have been worse.

The week passed slowly, and much to everyone's relief the war continued to keep its distance. On Friday morning, Edward and Peter left for school and Billy and Jeannie sat in the parlour, awaiting the arrival of the Child Welfare officer. She arrived at nine o'clock, and Beryl made the introductions. Mrs Pritchard was a stylish woman in her thirties, with light brown hair that matched the colour of her brown check over-blouse and pleated skirt.

As Beryl waved them all off at the gate, she wished she could have taken them instead. It didn't seem right that they should be taken to attend their mother's funeral by a complete stranger. It was ridiculous, she knew, but as soon as they were out of sight she began to miss them.

The journey to London was long and boring. There was nothing to do and not much to look at, and Mrs Pritchard made no attempt to encourage conversation. Jeannie dozed and Billy took a scrap of paper and a stub of pencil from his pocket and tried to draw his mother. For some reason the sketch came out looking more like Beryl.

By the time the train hauled itself into Liverpool Street Station, both children felt tired and irritable, but the journey wasn't over yet. A short bus-ride took them through the bustling city and into more familiar surroundings, and they now welcomed the distractions. A lot had changed since the children had been evacuated. Sandbags had been piled high in front of the town hall, and brick-built air-raid shelters had appeared on street corners. The lampposts and trees sported white stripes at their bases, and normally-red postboxes had been painted yellow.

'What's that in aid of?' asked Billy in his usual blunt fashion.

'The boxes have been coated with a special paint,' Mrs Pritchard explained. 'In the event of a gas attack, the paint will change colour and that will tell us to put our masks on.'

'Oh.'

The children were glued to the window of the bus, looking for anything or anyone they knew. They finally alighted outside a greengrocer's shop, and Mrs Pritchard led them down a quiet side road. They stopped outside a small terraced house.

The children heard a baby crying inside, and saw a curtain twitch suspiciously at the front bay window just seconds after Mrs Pritchard knocked at the door.

A moment later the door opened and a young woman appeared in the doorway, holding a tearful baby in her arms. The two women exchanged a few words, and then Billy and Jeannie were gently pushed into the dim, narrow hallway, with the promise that Mrs Pritchard would return shortly to take them to the funeral.

Mrs Brown's house was neat and tidy, and to the children's relief she turned out to be a friendly soul. She chattered constantly to the pair and quickly eased some of their misgivings. Her husband was away in the navy, she said, and though he'd tried to persuade her to swap London for the country, taking their eight-month old daughter, Peggy, with her, she was reluctant to leave her parents, who lived nearby. She said she took in other people's children as and when the need arose.

'Baby's teething,' she added. 'Here, can you see?'

She held the baby down low enough for them to see the baby's two tiny teeth. Billy wasn't especially interested, but Jeannie took to the little girl at once and offered one finger to her little, out-stretched hand. The baby grabbed at it, and Jeannie squealed with delight.

'She must like you, Jeannie,' said Mrs Brown. 'She doesn't take to everyone, you know.'

She walked over to a pink wicker bassinette in the corner of the kitchen and set the baby gently onto the mattress.

'I've got a little package for you two,' she said suddenly. 'Mrs Pritchard went through all your mother's effects and took out all the things she thought you might like or need.'

As Mrs Brown disappeared into another

room, Billy and Jeannie looked at each other. When the woman came back in, she was carrying a brown paper parcel tied with string. She offered it to Billy, who took it warily and began to pick at the knot.

'Here, let's get some scissors,' said Mrs Brown.

She opened a drawer by the sink and cut the string for him with one quick snip. 'Put it on the table,' she said, 'in case everything falls out.'

Billy carefully unwrapped the package, not at all sure what he was going to find inside. Folded into a neat pile were the children's few items of clothing, on top of which sat a long manila envelope.

'What's in it, Billy?' asked Jeannie, straining to look inside as her brother picked up the envelope and tore it open.

There were a few papers inside, an insurance policy, their birth certificates and medical cards, his mother's watch, her wedding ring and several old photos. The latter he fanned out in front of them.

He didn't recognise the first two pictures. One was of an austere-looking lady dressed in Victorian costume, the other of a man posing beside a large hound. In the next one he saw himself at the age of five. It had been taken in the back garden. The next one was of Jeannie, sitting on their mother's knee.

The one that claimed Billy's attention,

however, was a studio portrait of a man dressed smartly in a dark suit and tie. There was a broad, disarming smile on his face.

'That man looks like you!' Jeannie hissed excitedly.

Billy had already seen the likeness.

He turned the photograph over. An inscription had been scrawled on the back. It said:

To Ada,
With love
April 1929

He studied the photograph again. There was no denying the resemblance between them. The same dark eyes, the same olive skin, the same mouth, the same thick, dark hair.

He looked at the inscription again. 1929. The year before he was born.

'Who is he, Billy?' asked Jeannie.

'I think it's Dad,' he replied in a near-whisper.

Jeannie reached for the photograph. 'Let me see,' she said, studying the man's face. 'I *said* he looked like you!'

'I know,' he replied, feeling proud of the fact. 'Here, better let me put all these somewhere safe.'

He gathered up the contents of the package, pausing briefly to slip the ring onto his little finger. His mother hadn't worn it for years, but because his father had bought it, he knew he would treasure it.

His father, he thought. His *dad*.

He wondered if Dad would attend the funeral.

He didn't.

Aside from Billy, Jeannie and Mrs Pritchard, the only other mourner was Uncle George. A stocky man of about average height, with a pink face and a bald head, he seemed much quieter than the children remembered, almost washed-out. There was none of his usual swagger. Instead he cried throughout the service, and afterwards knelt before the children and said that he was sorry, that he hadn't meant for things to turn out the way they had, that he'd loved their mother, that he'd always loved her and wouldn't have hit her at all had it not been for the drink.

The children didn't really understand what he was talking about, and Mrs Pritchard never gave him the chance to explain himself more clearly. She said, 'I don't think the children need to hear any of that, Mr Hesketh.'

He regained his feet, turned his pork pie fedora nervously by its skinny brim. 'Ah, no. No, I suppose not. It's just that if I hadn't–'

'Quite,' said Mrs Pritchard. 'Now, if you'll excuse us…'

158

He nodded, his lips beginning to twitch again. 'Goodbye, children. You … you w-won't hate your Uncle George, will you?'

They didn't know of any reason why they should.

Returning to Mrs Brown's, they picked at their tea. They had no real appetite, and the events of the day had worn them both out. Eventually Mrs Brown said, 'Come on, you two. Go and get your nightclothes on, and then I'll make you some nice warm milk.'

A little less than half an hour later, they were tucked up in a single bed in Mrs Pritchard's spare room. Billy had hardly let the brown envelope out of his sight, and he now placed it beneath his pillow – but not before he'd taken another good look at his father's photograph.

Chapter Fifteen

Time Off for Bad Behaviour

At last the war began to hot up. On 14th September the Royal Navy sent a German submarine, *U-39,* to the bottom of the Atlantic. Three days later the Germans sunk *HMS Courageous* off the coast of Ireland. The Russians – uneasy allies of Nazi Germany – invaded Poland from the east and linked up with German forces at Brest-Litovsk, on the Russian-Polish border, and on 20th September, the RAF fought its first engagement with the *Luftwaffe*.

In Little Asham, however, life went on much the same as usual. The children attended school, with Billy's class still taking its lessons outdoors, and then spent all their free time either at the abbey or in the overgrown orchard. In the evenings they sat with Beryl in the parlour and listened to the radio, or played games. Billy, however, kept mostly to himself.

Try as he might, he just couldn't understand why his father hadn't attended his mum's funeral. Didn't he *want* to remember all the things he'd loved about her before she went to Heaven? Maybe he didn't even know she was *dead*. Maybe he was too busy spying on the Germans.

Or maybe he just didn't *care*.

Much as he hated to admit it, this last explanation seemed the most likely. After all, he'd left them once because he didn't want to be with them anymore. Why would he come back now, just for Mum's funeral?

During every private moment he studied his father's photograph and tried to understand what he and Jeannie had done that was so bad that he'd decided to turn his back on them. But try as he might, he couldn't think of a single thing.

In any case, he'd argue to himself, things were *different* now. He and Jeannie were that much older, for a start. These days they *never* did anything bad. Well, nothing *really* bad, anyway. They were *good* children now, and they'd be even better if only he'd come back and start being their dad again.

But he knew the chances of that happening were slim, at best. And maybe that was just as well. After all, who wanted a dad who'd already walked out on you once? You'd never know where you stood with a man like that. One wrong word and he'd more than likely walk out on you all over again.

In those private moments, when his thoughts drew him back to this same, inevitable conclusion, he would clench his fists and clamp his jaw and try not to cry but cry anyway.

Because he *loved* his dad.

He *hated* his dad.

But above all, he *needed* his dad.

It was on the morning of Wednesday the twentieth that Billy's frustrations finally boiled to the surface.

After a class recitation of the alphabet and readings from a book of poetry, playtime came and the children inside the school began to hurry out to join those already in the field.

As had become their custom, Edward and Peter waited at the corner of the school building until Miss Ferguson dismissed her class, then all three boys retired to a shady spot on the edge of the field. Billy, still largely in a world of his own, only half-listened as Peter told him that Edward had been appointed book monitor. It was hard to get excited about news like that, even on a good day.

Jeannie, who never liked to stray far from her brother, was playing about thirty yards away. On their first morning at school, she'd made friends with a shy, lisping girl called Ann Smith, who had dark, wavy hair and a petite, doll-like appearance. The two had become inseparable, and had now settled down to make daisy chains together.

They were quite content in each other's company until two shadows suddenly fell across them. When they looked up, they found Alan Windom and Lenny Cornford blocking out the autumn sunshine. A moment later Alan swatted the daisies out of Jeannie's hand, sending them through the air in a yellow-white shower.

'Oi, *you!*' Jeannie yelped crossly. 'You leave us alone!'

The sound of her raised voice brought Billy out of his daydream, and he immediately jumped to his feet with Edward and

Peter not far behind him. One glance had told him all he needed to know about what was happening, and he quickly set off in the bullies' direction.

When he was close enough he called, 'Why don't you leave my sister alone an' go pick on someone your own size?'

Alan turned just as Billy planted himself a few feet away, his fists clenched and a scowl knitting his eyebrows together.

With a slack grin, Alan reached out and gave Billy's right shoulder a hard shove. Billy staggered back a pace, then caught his balance and said, 'I'm warnin' you...'

'What're you going to do, Billy-Goat?' smirked Alan. 'Go crying to your *mummy?*'

Something about the word, about the way he *said* the word, made something inside Billy snap, and he threw himself at the bigger boy and they went down in a heap.

Edward tried to grab Billy's arm and haul him off, but he was a whirlwind of movement as he straddled the wailing troublemaker and kept hitting him, left, right, left, right.

Children immediately came running from every direction, eager to watch the contest.

The two boys fell apart, hastily climbed as far as their knees and started trading wild, largely ineffectual blows. Billy's hair stuck out at odd angles and his cheeks had grown bright scarlet. He took a punch on the chin

163

and that only fuelled his anger, and he fought back even harder.

Now they were back on their feet, and Alan Windom began to understand what it must be like to have a tiger by the tail. Though younger and smaller, Billy was not in the least bit intimidated by him. In fact, not even the combined might of Edward Price and that other vaccie kid, Peter Something, could drag him off.

Around them the other children were screaming them on. *'Fight! Fight! Fight!'* The noise was deafening. Alan was bleeding from one nostril, Billy from a split in his bottom lip. They were flushed and sweaty, breathing hard, dishevelled.

And then, as if from out of nowhere, the booming voice of Mrs Abbott cut through the yelling of the excited onlookers, through the hammer of blood in the combatants' ears, and the children quickly parted to allow their headmistress to sweep into the makeshift arena and call for calm.

'Alan Windom! Billy Curtis! How *dare* you behave in such a fashion! Stop this at once!'

The two boys fell apart, but not before Alan aimed one last, spiteful kick at Billy's left ankle.

'That will be *quite* enough of that!' bellowed Mrs Abbott. 'My room, both of you, *now!*'

Billy looked up at her. He knew he should

obey. But all at once he felt like a trapped, helpless animal. His life had been turned upside-down, not once, not twice but *three* times now, and he was sick of it, scared of waiting for it to happen a fourth and then a fifth time. He treated Mrs Abbott to one final glare and then made a run for it, pushing through the surrounding children and heading for the sanctuary of the trees and hedges at the bottom of the field.

The children started yelling again. Dimly he heard Mrs Abbott calling his name. Ignoring her, he kept running, not once looking back, not once *daring* to. All that mattered now was that he get away: from the school, from the teachers, from the other pupils – even Edward, Peter and Jeannie.

He reached a point where the hedge gave way to a five-bar gate, and flung himself onto and then over it into the lane beyond, where he paused for a moment to steady himself and catch his breath.

Voices reached him from further down the lane, and he stiffened, then relaxed. On the way to school that morning they'd passed several workmen in khaki overalls, clearing bushes at the junction of the lane. It was the workmen he could hear now.

Angrily he dashed the tears from his eyes and started running in the general direction of Holly Cottage. The workmen looked up

165

as he drew nearer and one of them asked him if he was all right. He made no attempt to reply, just kept running.

At last the cottage blurred into view, but that was not his destination. He ran past, turned his foot in an old wheel-rut twenty yards further on and he went down hard. He wasn't so much sobbing now as moaning, and he couldn't seem to stop.

Finally he sat up. He'd grazed one knee and it was bleeding sluggishly. He'd also scratched his elbows in the fall.

He climbed back to his feet and looked over his shoulder, down the lane, but there was no-one in pursuit. In any case, he'd almost reached his destination now, so he limped on, somehow exhausted beyond measure by the sudden, tumultuous rush of his emotions.

As he climbed the stile and jogged the final two hundred yards to the moss-covered steps of the abbey, a breeze picked up and sent a shiver down his spine. Reaching the abbey wall, he pressed his palms to its uneven surface and immediately felt better, for in his mind *this* was his home now, the closest thing he had to one.

His relief was short-lived. Sensing movement away to his left, he spun quickly. A rabbit fifteen feet away sat back on its haunches, watching him curiously through big, saucer-like eyes the colour of wet coal. Relaxing again, Billy squatted down on the top step and held out his hand to the animal, but it turned and hopped away on long hind legs.

He straightened up again. The sun sent shafts of sunlight down across the ruined walls and cast bent and distorted shadows over the grass within. Billy sensed the mysticism of the place, its magic.

Slowly he walked through the tall grass until he came to the familiar tumble of the fallen spire where he and his friends spent so much time. He wiped the back of his hand across his forehead, then his eyes, then his nose. At last he climbed up onto the spill of masonry and once again sprawled out on the stone, feeling the sun on his skin.

He glanced down at the daisies growing at the base of the rocks, and again thought of Jeannie. That's how this trouble had started, with Jeannie and Ann picking daisies! He hoped his sister would be all right. Peter and Edward would look after her.

His eyes suddenly caught sight of something else in the grass and he sat up quickly. He jumped down, wincing at the pain in his grazed knee, then bent and picked up the object.

It was a cigarette card.

Billy stood up and looked around warily, as if he expected its owner to be standing nearby. He turned it over. It showed a picture of a wildcat, with the usual explanatory text on the reverse. But it was brand new! Not dirty or weathered, but brand new! And that could only mean one thing.

Someone else had been here.

Carefully he picked a path through the grass and round to the far side of the abbey ruin, searching for any further sign of the intruder. The shadow of the abbey's great north wall covered the grass like a huge grey blanket, but there was nothing else to be found.

He put the card into his pocket and wandered back to his rocky perch.

Peter hadn't been able to believe his eyes when Billy tore across the field and disappeared over the gate into the lane beyond. Mrs Abbott had called after him, but Billy had just kept running.

Around her, the other children had started cheering with excitement. Unlike Peter and Edward, they didn't really understand what had just happened, or why. Mrs Abbott had clapped her hands smartly to restore order, then called for everyone to line up in front of their respective teacher – except for Alan Windom, that was. He stood facing the wall until Mrs Abbott finally marched him into her office.

Jeannie spent the rest of the afternoon wondering tearfully what had happened to make her brother run away, and whether or not he would ever come back to her. Ann was a great comfort.

Edward and the rest of his class sat reading in silence until Mrs Abbott reappeared with Alan. Alan was blushing furiously and looked well and truly cowed. Mrs Abbott beckoned to Edward and he hurried to join her in the foyer.

'Do you have any idea where Billy Curtis might have gone?' she asked.

'I'm not sure, miss…' he hedged.

'Do you think he might have gone back to your mother?'

'He might have, I suppose.'

'You had better go and find out, then,' she decided. 'We can't have the boy running loose in that state.'

'No, miss.'

Edward left school and turned his step toward home. On the way he came to the spot at which the workmen had been toiling in the lane, their large, open-backed lorry parked by the roadside.

The five men were now sitting on the grass verge, eating sandwiches and drinking tea. Their shovels lay nearby.

As Edward hurried past, he saw that the lorry held a great pile of wooden signposts. He frowned, realising that the workmen were taking all the village signs down.

Deep in thought, he carried on towards the cottage. He hoped his mother wasn't around to see him, because he had no intention of going home. Instead he hurried past and continued on toward the abbey.

He reached the stile, climbed over into the field and then ran the remainder of the way up the steps. He wasn't at all surprised when he found Billy on the rocky outcrop. He *was* surprised, however, to find him soundly asleep.

He crept closer, not wanting to make his friend jump, and caught sight of Billy's grazed knee and elbows. He sat down beside the boy, deciding to wait until he woke up of his own accord. But Billy opened his eyes almost immediately, and when he sat up without warning, it was Edward who jumped.

'I thought you were asleep!' he cried. 'Look at your knee! What happened?'

'I fell over,' said Billy.

'I guessed that! But what happened at *school?*'

Billy countered that with a question of his own. 'Is Mrs Abbott angry?'

Edward gave the question a moment's thought. 'I don't think so. I think she was more worried than angry. She gave Alan a right old telling-off, though! Then she asked me if I knew where you might be, and I said I did, so she sent me to find you.'

'Is Jeannie all right?'

'I think so.'

'It didn't upset her too much, did it? Me

running off, I mean?'

'Well, she'll be happy to see you again.'

A new thought occurred to him. 'Edward,' he said seriously. 'Someone else has been here!'

'*What?*'

Billy fumbled in his pocket and brought out the card, which he placed on the rock in front of him.

'Where did you find it?' asked Edward, picking the card up and inspecting it.

'Down there, in the tall grass. I looked all over, but I couldn't see anything else.'

'It's brand new, isn't it?' said Edward, handing it back to Billy. 'It'll go well in your collection. But I wonder who's been here?'

'Well, whoever he is, let's hope he doesn't come back again. This is *our* place!'

Edward gave him a searching look. 'We'd better be getting back,' he said.

'What, so Mrs Abbott can give me the cane?'

'I told you, she's more worried than annoyed,' said Edward. 'She knows you've had a bad time of it.'

'She's bound to tell me off,' fretted Billy.

'Probably,' Edward agreed. 'But I think that's the worst you can expect.'

Billy gave it some thought. He really didn't want to go back. But what would happen to Jeannie, if she didn't have him to watch out for her?'

'Anyway,' said Edward, 'I think we should go home first and explain it all to my mum. Then maybe she can explain it all to Mrs Abbott.'

Billy still didn't like the idea, but he didn't really see that he had much choice. Reluctantly he climbed to his feet and then reached down to pull Edward up as well.

'Come on, then,' he said, his tone that of a condemned man.

Beryl was in the garden when the two boys slipped through the side gate. She turned suddenly, her face registering surprise.

'Hello, you two,' she said. 'What are–?'

Then she saw how dishevelled Billy was, the fact that he'd caught his knee and been crying.

'What happened?' she asked urgently.

'Billy had a fight!' said Edward. 'Alan Windom started picking on Jeannie and–'

'I sorted him out,' said Billy. 'An' then I ran away!'

Beryl frowned. 'Ran away?'

Edward nodded. 'Mrs Abbott sent me to find him,' he explained.

'Billy, that was a very bad thing to do,' Beryl began.

Impulsively, Edward said, 'What Alan Windom did was even worse.'

She looked at him. 'What do you mean by that?'

Edward looked at the ground and said quietly, 'He made a remark about Billy's mum.'

Beryl was silent for a moment. She stared at Billy for a long moment, and he prepared himself for the worst. Then, at last, she reached out and to his surprise gave him a hug. 'Oh, Billy,' she said, sounding more concerned than angry. 'Come on, let's go into the kitchen and get you cleaned up.'

Inside, she boiled some water and poured it into a small dish. Billy sat quietly at the table. After adding a little cold, Beryl produced some cotton wool from the cupboard and soaked it. She knelt in front of him and gently bathed, then dried, his cuts. At last she smiled and said, 'Right – you'll do.'

'Do I have to go back to school now?' asked Billy.

Beryl said, 'The sooner you go back and face the music, the better. But I think tomorrow's soon enough, don't you?'

The relief on Billy's face was obvious. 'What about Edward?' he asked.

'Edward can go back and tell Mrs Abbott that you're safe and sound and back home with me,' she said. 'Here, Edward, I'll write her a note.'

Edward looked crestfallen at having to return to school, but did his best to hide it.

Keeping a straight face, Beryl added casually, 'I'll also tell her that I need you to run some errands for me, Edward, so make sure you come straight home again, won't you?'

His little face was a picture. 'Yes, Mum! I will!'

'Then we'll all go and meet Jeannie and Peter from school,' she concluded. 'And *you*, Billy Curtis, can apologise to Mrs Abbott for your behaviour.'

Chapter Sixteen

Ghost or Trespasser?

As soon as he delivered his mother's note to Mrs Abbott, Edward headed back to Holly Cottage at a run, anxious not to miss a moment of his free afternoon with Billy. He'd run all the way to school and now seemed intent on running all the way back home – a fact which didn't go unnoticed by the workmen in the lane.

'Blimey,' noted one of the men, leaning on his shovel. 'I wish I had half your energy, mate.'

Edward slowed down. 'Eh? I'm sorry?'

'Is there a party goin' on, or summat?' the workman asked. He showed Edward a near-toothless grin. 'You kids have been racing backwards and forwards along here all mornin'.'

The penny finally dropped. 'Oh, no. No party. We just came home early from school, that's all.'

The workman suddenly sobered and asked quietly, 'Is the other lad all right? Las' time I saw him, he looked a bit upset.'

'Oh. He's all right now. He cut his knee, but my mum fixed it.'

'Good for her.'

'What are you *doing*?' Edward asked suddenly. 'Why are you taking down all the signposts?'

The workman shrugged. 'It's the war, see,' he said, as if that explained everything. ''Appen the Germans invade, they won't know where anything is, will they? That'll slow the beggars down.'

'I suppose so,' muttered Edward.

'Mind you,' said another workman, coming over. 'They've got to *land* before we can confuse 'em, and that'll be easier said than done after they finish putting the barbed wire up along Fenby beach.'

At three o'clock, Beryl, Edward and Billy went to meet Peter and Jeannie from school. By the time they arrived, several women had already congregated by the gate and were chatting among themselves. A few minutes later the door of the schoolhouse finally swung open and children of all ages came rushing down the steps.

Peter appeared with Jeannie trotting along beside him. Jeannie, of course, was delighted to see her brother and, much to Billy's embarrassment, flung her arms around him. Peter was more curious to know just where he'd gone after leaving school, but that would have to wait. Beryl was adamant that he must go in and apologise to Mrs Abbot first.

Whatever he'd been expecting – *dreading* was a better word – Billy was in for another very pleasant surprise. After mumbling his apology, Mrs Abbott seemed to thaw towards him and reminded him gently that, in the event of any trouble with another child, he must always seek out and tell one of the teachers, and never, *ever* try to settle a problem by violent means.

That didn't make a lot of sense to Billy, because the grown-ups in Britain had a problem with the grown-ups in Germany and settling that sounded like it was going to be pretty violent.

He didn't say that, of course. He just nodded and looked suitably sheepish, and Mrs Abbott, being all too familiar with Alan Windom's nasty nature, and having discovered the circumstances leading up to the fight, suggested they start afresh the following day.

Later that afternoon, Peter asked Billy if

he'd been scared going up to the abbey all by himself.

'I didn't really think about it,' he replied honestly. 'I mean, the sun was out, and everything just looked so ... nice.'

'He was sound asleep when I found him!' laughed Edward.

'Yeah,' he said. 'But before I fell asleep, look what I found!'

He produced the cigarette card from his pocket and showed it to Peter.

'Wow! Where did you find it?'

'Right by the abbey, in the grass! An' you know what *that* means, don't you?'

'That someone else has been there,' breathed Peter.

They began to walk slowly down the lane. It was very quiet, because the workmen had finished for the day.

'I wonder who he was,' mused Peter. 'Do many of the villagers go to the abbey, Edward?'

'Not that I know of,' admitted Edward.

'Well,' said Peter, 'maybe we should make it our business to find out!'

Billy's eyes widened at the prospect. 'You're on!' he said.

On Saturday morning Beryl gathered up the post and took it through to the kitchen. There was a letter for Peter, which he more or less tore open as soon as it was presented to him.

'Mum's coming to see me!' he cried excitedly once he'd finished reading it.

'That's lovely, Peter,' said Beryl. 'When is she coming?'

He hastily re-read the page. 'Um... She says she'll be catching the two o'clock train on Friday.' He looked up. 'Do you know where she can stay?'

Beryl considered. 'Well, the village is quite full at the moment, but I'm sure we'll find somewhere.'

She was thinking about Jack's old workroom upstairs, which had remained more or less untouched since his death. She couldn't remember the last time she'd gone in there. It had always held too many memories.

After breakfast, Billy suggested they go up to the abbey, just in case the owner of the cigarette card had made another visit. They were almost to the stile when they caught the drone of an aircraft in the distance.

'It's coming this way!' yelled Edward.

Together, they climbed onto the stile and eagerly scanned the clear blue sky, but when they finally spotted the plane, it was just a tiny dot high above them.

Disappointed, Edward jumped down into the tall grass with Billy, Peter and Jeannie following closely behind, and together they ran full pelt toward the abbey steps. Several minutes later, after a thorough and fruitless inspection of the area, they made their way back to the cottage.

They spent the rest of the morning in Edward's bedroom, where they cleared the small table of model aeroplanes and then tried to construct a car from a Meccano set. They soon became engrossed in their work, for it was fiddly and demanding, but after about half an hour they were disturbed by a series of low, dragging sounds coming from a room further along the landing.

Curiosity finally got the better of Edward, and he went out onto the landing to find the door to Dad's old workroom standing ajar.

'Oh!' said Beryl, turning at the soft creak of a loose floorboard. She glanced around, knowing that it had been a long time since either of them had visited the room. 'I thought I'd have a clear out,' she said.

The room was full of everything his father had collected over the years, including a vast library of books. There was a single bed with a bare mattress, a small, handsomely-made tallboy and a large, heavy-looking trunk, its lid now open to display a wide variety of tools. Along one wall stood a table that had doubled as a workbench, and beneath this, a large wooden box holding different lengths and thicknesses of wood. Incredibly, there was still a smattering of sawdust under the bench, and a saw lay, just as it had been left years before, on top.

Beryl hadn't wanted to disturb anything after Jack passed away, so she had left all this almost as a shrine to his memory. Even now, it was difficult not to imagine him standing there, strong and well-built, making something or other from a length of old timber, sawing here, carving there, then proudly showing her the finished product.

But Beryl felt different about things now. Jack was gone, and there was no bringing him back, except in memory.

Edward watched from the doorway, surprised by what he saw. His mother turned to smile at him. 'I'm going to turn this into a spare bedroom,' she said. 'That way, Peter's mum can stay here with us.'

'Gosh,' breathed Edward.

By late morning the sun began to struggle through some low-lying cloud. With their metal car completed and standing on the small table in Edward's bedroom, the children decided to take another stroll up to the abbey.

This time, a low mist hung like a shroud over the ruins. It created an eerie scene, and they weren't in quite such a hurry to venture any further than the stile, where they sat astride the topmost rung. The damp air held an almost artificial silence. There was no birdsong, no breeze, just a vaguely disturbing stillness.

The colours of autumn were now well and

truly painted. Fallen leaves provided a red and gold carpet for the lane, and the trees stood bare and misshapen. At last, somewhere high above them, a blackbird performed his song. It echoed mournfully in the stillness.

A sudden movement stirred the grass beyond the stile and caught their attention. A large rabbit hopped into the clearing and sat washing himself, alert to every sound and movement around him.

And then, suddenly–

Edward saw it first, an almost indistinct shape that was a slightly darker grey than the mist, hovering on the top-most step of the abbey, beneath the tall arch.

The breath caught in his throat.

'*Th-there!*' he managed at last.

When the others made no immediate response, he realised that he was still watching the rabbit. Not taking his eyes off the figure in the archway, he jabbed Peter in the side and when Peter looked up, he pointed to the shape.

Billy and Jeannie looked that way, too.

'*Crumbs!*' breathed Peter.

It was definitely the shape of a man. It seemed to move forward, descend the mist-covered steps, then stop in a swirl of fog, hover in the archway for a few seconds and then vanish back into the ruins.

Jeannie clutched Billy's arm and murmured, 'I wanna go home…'

'*Shhh!*'

They sat rooted to the spot, mouths open and eyes staring. Then Edward whispered, 'Di … di … did you see *that?*'

Peter managed a jittery nod.

All they could see around the archway now was mist, swirling lazily. The ghost, or figure or whatever it was, was nowhere to be seen.

Without warning, Billy suddenly hopped down into the wet grass of the field and hissed, '*Come on!*'

Peter's jaw dropped open. 'What? Go over *there? Now?* Are you mad?'

'Maybe,' admitted Billy. 'But we said we were goin' to find out who or what that thing is, and now's our chance!'

It was, of course, the last thing the others wanted to do. But even Jeannie knew they couldn't let Billy do all the investigating on his own. Besides, there was safety in numbers … wasn't there?

They approached the abbey with almost comical caution. The mist muffled every sound, even their own soft footfalls. Closer they went to the ruins, and then closer still, but they neither saw nor heard a thing.

But then–

There it was again, a ghostly apparition drifting through the far-most arch, until it vanished back into the mist!

Peter suddenly realised that he was hanging onto Edward's shirt-tail, and he swallowed noisily.

'I don't know about you,' he croaked, 'but I've seen enough. Can we go now?'

Billy shook his head. He wanted to know just what that thing was. So he crept on, through the empty, roofless, floorless abbey, and with no real option, the others followed behind.

There! Again!

The figure seemed to float across the aperture in the north wall, only to stop without warning, and appear to turn. It was for all the world as if it sensed that it was being spied upon.

A moment later their suspicion was confirmed. The ghost raised its arms and started toward them.

Billy yelled, *'Leg it!'*

The others needed no second urging. Obeying pure, blind instinct, they turned and ran for the abbey steps, slipping and sliding on the wet grass, and once there they threw themselves out into the field and ran for the stile, not once daring to look back for fear of what they might see.

Not until they were safely back in the lane did Billy chance a backward glance. There was nothing to see, just a flurry of breeze-blown leaves scurrying across the steps like startled mice.

Chapter Seventeen

Food for Thought

Evelyn Murray finished brushing her wavy auburn hair and then went over to the double bed, upon which sat her small case. She checked the contents one last time, ticking each item off her mental list in turn – a nightdress, two changes of clothes, spare clothes for Peter and a few cheap presents she'd managed to get for the other children.

This morning she'd had another letter from Tom – well, more of a note, really, after the censors had finished with it. But at least he was well. She had sat down and written a hasty reply, not wanting to leave it until she returned from Norfolk. She could write a longer letter then, and get Peter to write a little something, too, while she was away. That would really please Tom.

She carried the case downstairs, added some writing paper and an envelope from the walnut bureau in the front room, then glanced at the Westminster Chime clock on the mantelpiece, which had been a wedding present from Tom's sister. It was a little after nine o'clock. By the time she walked through to the bus stop and caught the bus to Liverpool Street, she'd be just right for the train.

Thelma Barratt, her next door neighbour, was sweeping her path when Evelyn closed and locked the front door behind her. 'You can do mine when you're finished there!' Evelyn laughed.

Thelma laughed as well. She was a short, well-rounded woman with a dark, almost Mediterranean look. 'Mornin', Eve. You off to see young Peter now, are you?'

'Yes. Can't wait.'

'I'll bet. Give him a kiss from me.'

'I will.'

'And you mind that little one in there,' Thelma added, nodding toward her midriff. 'I'll keep an eye on things here for you, so don't worry.'

'Thanks, love. Anyway, I'd better dash, or I'll miss my bus.'

She reached the station in plenty of time, climbed aboard the train and pulled her navy cashmere coat around her. Now that the time had finally come, she could hardly wait to see Peter again. Had he grown? She hoped not, otherwise the clothes she was fetching for him would never fit! And what about his voice? What if he sounded like a right old carrot-cruncher every time he opened his mouth?

Just as a shrill whistle echoed around the

185

station and doors slammed shut up and down the length of the train, a young woman opened the heavy door beside her, holding a little girl by the hand.

'Is this train going to Norwich?' she asked breathlessly.

Evelyn nodded. 'Yes, it is. Here, let me help you.'

The woman lifted the toddler onto the step and Evelyn picked her up and sat her on the seat beside her. Next came a weighty suitcase, then the woman herself, heaving a sigh of relief as she sank into a seat on the other side of the child.

'Phwoar! I thought I was going to miss it!' the woman said as the train suddenly lurched into motion.

'Are you going away for long?' asked Evelyn, to be sociable.

'We're going to stay with my aunt in Norfolk. We would've gone sooner, but I didn't want to travel with all the evacuees. I've heard some terrible stories about them, you know.'

'Oh?'

'You know,' said the woman, dropping her voice to a confidential whisper. 'About the way they're being treated.'

Evelyn frowned. What was that supposed to mean? Peter had said he was being treated well, but were his postcards subject to censorship as well? Suddenly she started to fear the worst.

Not being used to travel, she found the journey tiring, and was glad when the train finally pulled into Little Asham station. With a farewell nod to her fellow passenger, she stepped down from the carriage and took a deep breath of sweet country air.

Outside the station she hesitated for a moment, wondering whether to take the left fork or the right. It was an impossible choice, because there were no signs to help her. In the end she decided to take the right fork, and ask directions if she didn't find the cottage she was looking for.

As she came within sight of the hump-back bridge ahead, she caught the sound of children playing on the gentle breeze. *They* certainly didn't sound as if they were being ill-treated.

A short, portly man in his fifties was bustling towards her from the other side of the bridge. He wore a black tin helmet upon which was painted the letter *W.* When she was close enough, Evelyn asked him if this was the right way to Holly Cottage.

He stopped and offered her a respectful salute. 'Holly Cottage, ma'am? Yes indeed. It's just a little further down the lane a-ways, on the left. You can't miss it.'

'Thank you.'

Glancing at her case, he asked, 'Staying long, are you?'

'Just the weekend.'

'You're from London,' he said. 'I recognise your accent.'

'Yes. My little boy's been evacuated here.'

'Well, he's in good hands, if he's staying at Holly Cottage.' Drawing himself up, he added importantly, 'My name's King, by the way. I'm the ARP warden for Little Asham. Can I help you with your case?'

'I can manage, thanks.'

'As you were, then. Enjoy your stay.'

When she finally reached Holly Cottage, she saw that it was everything she'd imagined it to be, from the neatly-thatched roof to the garden full of colourful flowers. She walked up the stone path and knocked lightly on the door, then took a step back. A moment later Beryl answered, smoothing down her long plaid skirt.

Evelyn smiled. 'Mrs Price, is it?'

'Peter's mother?' replied Beryl.

'Oh, Evelyn, please.'

The two women shook hands. 'In you come, Evelyn,' said Beryl, offering her own first name. She'd been expecting to feel more nervous than she actually was, but then she'd been following Cheeky Joe's advice about taking her recovery slow and steady, and it seemed to be paying dividends. She actually felt better now than she had in years. 'I expect you could do with a nice cup of tea.'

Evelyn stepped through the door and, gesturing to her case, said, 'Shall I leave this here?'

'Just put it by the stairs,' said Beryl. 'Here, let me take your coat, and then you can have a sit down.'

Evelyn went through to the parlour. She saw with no small relief that it looked extremely homely. 'You've got a lovely cottage here, Beryl,' she said. 'Oh, and thank you so much for looking after Peter.'

'Peter's no bother,' said Beryl. 'In fact, they all get on well together. All being of an age, I expect.'

She disappeared into the kitchen and came back a short time later carrying a tray of tea things and a plate of freshly-baked scones. 'How was your journey?' she asked.

'Long and tiring.'

'Peter can't wait to see you, of course.'

'And I can't wait to see *him.*'

'I can imagine,' smiled Beryl. 'He's a wonderful lad, Evelyn, so polite and well-spoken. You must be very proud of him.'

'Oh, I am.'

'It's the other two *I* worry about,' confessed Beryl.

Evelyn frowned. 'Billy and Jeannie, you mean?'

Beryl looked uncomfortable for a moment. 'How well do you know them?' she asked.

'Not well at all, really. We met them the

morning of the evacuation. They were all by themselves. I took pity on them and suggested they pal up with Peter.' Evelyn sipped her tea. 'Why?'

Beryl said quietly. 'Their mother died last week. She was hit by a car in the Blackout.'

Visibly shocked, Evelyn breathed, *'No!'* Then, 'What about their father?'

Beryl shook her head. 'By all accounts he walked out on them when they were just babies.'

'The poor little mites.'

'I don't know what's going to become of them,' sighed Beryl. 'If I had my way, they'd stay with me, but what the authorities decide to do is anyone's guess.'

Changing the subject, she asked, 'How are you getting on in London, anyway? It seems a lot worse there than it is here.'

'The nights are the worst,' said Evelyn. 'Especially when the air-raid sirens go off. It's a case of grab everything and run – well walk rather slowly, in my condition! And most of the time they're false alarms.'

Things certainly weren't looking good, though. Government forecasters were predicting the war to last for three years, and taxes were already rising to an unprecedented seven and six in the pound to pay for it.

'What about your husband?' asked Beryl. 'Are his letters getting through?'

'I've had a couple from him, just to say he's all right. He's out in France somewhere, with the Royal Engineers. What about yours?'

'Jack passed away three years ago,' Beryl said quietly.

'Oh. I *am* sorry,' said Evelyn. 'So you're all alone here, then? Apart from your son?'

'Yes. Jack was just getting the orchard up and running when he died. Apples, you know. Trouble is, apart from Edward picking a few for the neighbours, and the odd pie and sauce, the rest just rot on the trees. It's a waste, really. Sometimes I think it would be easier to sell off the land, but when it comes to it, well … it was Jack's dream, you see.'

'It must be very difficult for you,' Evelyn sympathised.

Beryl suddenly got to her feet. 'Come on, I'll show you around – that's if you feel up to it?'

'It'll be nice to stretch my legs after sitting for so long on the train.'

Evelyn fell in love with the garden. 'Oh, it's lovely,' she said. 'A bit different to my little terrace in London! Mind you, I've done wonders with the shelter they've given us.' She chuckled. 'Proper little palace, it is! I've even planted some flowers either side of the door!'

'Oh, that reminds me,' said Beryl. 'Did you arrange for anywhere to stay, after all?'

'No. I was hoping there might be a little

boarding house or someone with a spare room.'

'*I've* got a spare room,' said Beryl. 'So that settles *that*.'

'Oh, thank you, Beryl. That's a weight off my mind.'

'Come on, I'll show you,' Beryl said with a smile. She led her visitor back through to the narrow passage, picked up Evelyn's case and then climbed the stairs. 'I'm afraid you'll have to share it with a few odds and ends.'

'Oh, I think I can put up with that.'

As far as Evelyn was concerned, the spacious room was perfect. Beryl had transformed it from a dusty hobby room to a neat and tidy guest room. The tools had been consigned to the shed, the table-cum-workbench was covered in a pretty floral tablecloth, and the single bed now sported a beautiful crocheted bedspread.

'Just look at that view!' Evelyn gasped, crossing to the window.

Beryl came to stand beside her. 'That's the church at Fenby you can see in the distance,' she explained. 'And you can see the sea beyond.'

Evelyn leaned on the narrow window sill to get a better look.

'The abbey ruins are just over there, and of course Little Asham itself is over that way. I've been taking the children to church with me. I hope that's all right?'

'It's ever so good of you,' Evelyn said gratefully. 'It really is.'

She turned away from the window, feeling considerably happier about Peter now that she'd seen Beryl Price and Holly Cottage for herself.

They spent a pleasant afternoon together, and by the time they set out to collect the children from school, felt as if they'd known each other for years.

When they reached the school, Beryl suggested they wait in the lane opposite the school gate. Evelyn had fallen quiet now as anticipation began to grow within her. All at once all she could think about was Peter, of seeing him after so long and hugging him and spoiling him something rotten. Her throat tightened and her eyes misted just at the thought of it.

A few minutes later the door opened wide and children ran to the gates, laughing and shouting and waving, to be collected by their parents or guardians. Evelyn strained to spot Peter in the crowd, but he was nowhere to be seen. But then – yes, yes, it was *him!* She was *sure* it was him!

'*Peter!*' she called, and started to wave.

Peter had come out of school with Edward, Billy and Jeannie, but his attention had been fixed on the school gate, where he knew his mother would be waiting for him.

When he spotted her on the other side of the lane, his whole face lit up.

'*Mum!*'

Evelyn was like a child herself now, as she continued waving.

Peter broke into a run, pushing past everyone else in his haste to get to her. He blurred across the lane and threw himself at her, hugging her tight and never wanting to let her go.

'Mum,' he said again, his voice muffled by the material of her coat this time, and by a sudden rush of tears.

Evelyn, herself overcome with emotion, bent and kissed his head. 'Oh, love,' she said, 'I've missed you!'

At last she held him at arm's-length and said, 'I do believe you've grown taller!'

Edward, Billy and Jeannie ran up just then. Jeannie made straight for Beryl, calling as she came, 'Mu – uh ... Mrs Price!'

'Hello, angel.'

'Guess what?' asked Jeannie. 'We learned how to *knit* today! We're going to knit scarves and things for the men in the army!'

'Are you, indeed?'

Evelyn looked down at Billy and said quietly, 'Hello, love.'

Billy gave her a shy smile, but this was no time to stand on ceremony. Impulsively Evelyn pulled him to her and hugged him tight. Even now he wasn't used to such shows of affection, but he had to admit, if only to himself, that they were quite nice.

As they all turned their steps for home, Jeannie automatically slipped her hand into Beryl's.

'You didn't tell us your mum was pregnant,' said Billy.

'Billy!' said Beryl.

Peter shrugged. 'I forgot.'

'Well, what do you want? A brother or a sister?' asked Edward.

'A brother,' Peter replied immediately.

Jeannie pulled a face. '*I'd* like a sister,' she said.

Billy gave her a playful nudge. 'Well,' he allowed. 'Sisters ain't so bad.'

That teatime was a noisy but joyous affair. The children were full of chatter, anxious to tell Evelyn all about their adventures in and around the cottage. The nights were drawing in now, and by six o'clock they were all settled in the parlour, the children waiting patiently as Evelyn delved into her bag and brought out toys for each of them.

The boys' gifts were identical – Frog Mark IV Interceptor Fighter kits. Once assembled, the aeroplanes could be flown by using the winder in the side to tighten an elastic band that was attached to the propeller. Of the three, Edward was most in his element, and it wasn't long before it became a race to see who could make up their kit first.

Evelyn presented Jeannie with a baby doll, complete with a pink hand-knitted romper suit. It was clear by her reaction that Jeannie had been starved of such gifts in the past.

The two women sat back in comfortable silence, Beryl with her knitting, Evelyn with her eyes closed.

'You look as if you could do with an early night,' noted Beryl.

Evelyn sat forward suddenly. 'Actually, I've just been thinking,' she replied. 'Tell me to mind my own business if you like, but I really think you *should* try to get the orchard up and running again. After all, you've got *three* lads to help you now.'

Beryl grimaced. 'Oh, I don't know. It needs a fair bit of work done to it. It hasn't really been tended since Jack...'

'But it *could* be done,' Evelyn pressed enthusiastically.

Beryl said no more, but once the idea took root in her mind, she found it difficult to stop thinking about it. Evelyn was right. It *could* be done. And best of all, she could certainly think of no finer monument to Jack than being able to turn his long-cherished dream into a reality.

Evelyn awoke to the sound of children's voices drifting up through the partially-open window. It was still quite early, half-past seven, according to her bedside clock.

196

She got up, grabbed her dressing-gown from the chair and then made her way down the stairs and through to the kitchen, where she put the kettle on to boil. The scullery door was ajar, and she winced as her bare feet made contact with the cold flagstones. She poked her head outside, but the children had strayed beyond the garden.

She returned to the kitchen and made the tea, then took one cup upstairs and knocked lightly on Beryl's bedroom door.

Beryl woke with a start and sat up quickly. 'Gracious!' she exclaimed. 'What time is it?'

'Just you stay where you are,' advised Evelyn. 'It's only twenty to eight.' She put the cup on Beryl's bedside cabinet, beside a small, framed photograph of a man she took to be Jack.

'I'll get the breakfast started,' began Beryl, clearly flustered.

'No, you won't!' Evelyn replied firmly. 'Have your tea. There's no need to rush. I'll do the children's breakfasts, and then we can enjoy ours. It's the least I can do after all you've done for Peter.'

'I must have slept heavy,' Beryl murmured half to herself. 'I had such strange dreams.'

As she reached for her cup, she wondered how long it had been since she'd last had tea in bed. Jack always used to fetch her a cup every morning.

'That was it!' she said suddenly.

'That was what?' asked Evelyn, at the door.

'My dream. Jack was in the orchard, and there were apples everywhere we looked!'

Evelyn smiled down at her. 'You *see*,' she said knowingly. 'Someone's trying to *tell* you something.'

'I can hear someone calling!' said Jeannie, standing still in the long grass with her doll cradled in her arms. 'Listen!'

She looked up at Billy, who was struggling to retrieve his aeroplane from where it had become lodged in the lowermost branches of one of the trees. He gave the branch a vigorous shake and the plane finally tumbled back to earth.

They heard the call again.

Edward yelled, *'Coming!'* and started back toward the cottage, with Peter in tow. Billy and Jeannie soon caught up with them.

'Last one home's a scarecrow!' yelled Billy.

The children ran through the gap in the hedge and down the path, where Evelyn stood in the doorway, watching them come.

As they sat at the table, and Evelyn set about spooning porridge from a large enamel saucepan into four bowls, Edward glanced around with a look of concern on his face. 'Is Mum all right?' he asked.

'She's fine,' Evelyn assured him. 'She's just have a lay-in for a change. I daresay she'll be down in a minute.'

Sure enough, Beryl came into the kitchen a short while later, carrying her cup and saucer to the sink. 'That's what I like to see,' she said by way of greeting. 'Four children tucking into their food!'

'Mrs Price, can I show Mum the abbey ruins today?' asked Peter.

'You'd better ask your mum if she'd like to see them, first,' Beryl advised. 'She might not be up to all that walking.'

'Do you, Mum?' asked Peter. 'They're really good!'

'I'd love to,' said Evelyn.

An idea suddenly occurred to Beryl. 'I'll tell you what we'll do, then,' she said, and she could hardly believe that she was actually suggesting it. 'If you *do* feel up to it, Evelyn, we'll take a picnic and walk through to Fenby. Then you can see the sea, as well.'

There was a chorus of excited shouts from the children.

Chapter Eighteen

Get Ahead to Get a Hat

As soon as Beryl and Evelyn finished preparing and packing the picnic, the little group set off up the lane. It was now late September, but there was still enough of summer left to make it a perfect day for a stroll in the countryside.

Once, Jeannie stopped to look through an opening in the hedge at the Land Army girls working in the field beyond. 'Do you think Maude's over there?' she wondered aloud.

'Who's Maude, poppet?' asked Evelyn, coming to a halt beside her.

'She's in the Land Army,' Jeannie explained. '*And* she wears trousers!'

'Wears trousers!' echoed Evelyn, looking impressed. 'Well I *never!* Still, I expect she has to, working out in all weathers.' She glanced at Beryl. 'You've got to hand it to them, though, haven't you? Taking over the men's jobs like that.'

By this time the boys had reached the stile and were now seated side by side on the top rung.

'Well look at that!' Beryl observed with a

laugh. 'The three wise monkeys!'

'Come on, Mum!' yelled Peter.

'How on earth do you expect your mother to climb over *that?*' asked Beryl. 'You three go on ahead, and take Jeannie with you, if she wants to go. We'll watch you from here, then take a slow walk up the lane.'

'Come on, Jeannie!' shouted Billy.

'I'm staying here!' Jeannie called back. And to the two women she explained confidentially, 'There's a ghost in there. I've seen him.'

The two women and Jeannie carried on up the lane, which eventually gave way to a low fence beyond which a rising green field stretched far into the distance. The only sounds were the boys as they raced each other across the grass, and the occasional flutter of a disturbed bird.

The lane turned sharply to the left and then separated into a small junction. 'We're almost there, now,' said Beryl.

Two cottages stood off to their right, with identical white picket fences separating them from the lane. A chubby little Jack Russell ran up to the gate of one, yapping frantically, and Edward put a hand through the opening in order to pet the animal.

'This is Max,' Edward told the others. 'Hello, boy! I haven't seen you for a while, have I?'

Peter and Billy joined Edward at the gate.

The little terrier basked in all the attention. Jeannie, however, deliberately held back and pushed herself between Beryl and Evelyn.

'He won't hurt you, love,' Evelyn assured her.

'He *might*,' replied Jeannie.

'I wish *we* had a dog,' said Edward, casting a meaningful sideways glance at his mother.

'And I wish that I had a penny for every time I've heard you say that!' Beryl replied.

Edward pouted. *'Please?'*

'Who'd feed it, and take it for walks?'

'I will, Mum! I promise!'

Lowering her voice, Beryl confided to Evelyn, 'I know I'll give in to him some day. I mean, it's not as if I don't *like* dogs. We always had one when I was little.'

Up ahead, an enormous, muscular horse was pulling an old farm cart towards them. A solemn, dark-haired youth sat on the seat. They waited patiently on the grass verge until the cart drew level and then rumbled past.

They were approaching a more built-up area now, and when they turned the next corner, they found themselves in a small market square where stallholders were selling everything from fresh fruit and vegetables to fish caught that very morning off the coast of Fenby.

Edward stood still for a moment and took a deep sniff. 'I love the smell of wet fish!' he declared.

Billy, by contrast, immediately wrinkled up his nose. 'It's 'orrible!'

After buying a few things to take back with them, they crossed the village green, passed a row of tiny shops and cottages, then branched off down beside a quaint, pink-washed house, where the lane became no more than a thin, cobbled path.

A cool breeze swept towards them as they made their way out onto a narrow gravel walkway, where fishermen's huts stood like sentinels on the stony beach. Unfortunately, a makeshift fence now blocked the steps that led down to the sea, and a large red notice affixed to it read:

USE OF
BEACH
PROHIBITED

Billy and Jeannie stood in awe, having never seen the sea before. Grey waves crashed up over the shoreline and bubbled across the pebbles in a white froth before receding with a hiss to then do it all over again.

'I didn't know it looked like this!' exclaimed Billy.

Peter came up beside him. It had been a long time since he'd been to the seaside, and he too was entranced.

At last they made their way over to a long, open-fronted wooden hut with benches running along the back wall. 'At least we'll be sheltered from the worst of the wind here,' said Beryl, glad to sit down after their walk.

'It's a shame we can't go onto the beach,' Evelyn replied, sitting down next to her. 'Still, I suppose they know what they're doing. But being invaded from the sea … surely we'd see the Germans coming a mile off, if that's what they planned to do?'

'You'd think so, wouldn't you?' returned Beryl. 'We used to come here a lot, Jack and I. Edward was just a toddler, then, of course. Jack used to gather him up in his arms and pretend to throw him into the water. Do you remember that, Edward?'

Edward nodded. 'I remember kicking my shoe off once, and it landed in the sea! Dad had to roll his trousers up and go in after it!'

They all laughed.

'I've got a photo of him somewhere, holding up the shoe,' added Beryl.

'Do you remember that time we went to the seaside and I lost my teddy?' Peter chimed in.

'*Do* I!' Evelyn chuckled. 'I think we spent the rest of that day *looking* for him! You were inconsolable!'

'Did you find him?' asked Jeannie.

'Yes,' replied Peter. 'He was sitting in a rose bush, where I'd thrown him!'

A bearded man had been smoking a cigarette on a bench at the far end of the hut, a high-crowned grey fedora pulled low over his eyes, and the wide collar of his double-breasted, dark blue reefer jacket pulled up to shield his neck from the cool wind. Now he stood up and ground out his cigarette, then retrieved a cane from the bench and began to limp away.

He'd no sooner left the protection of the shelter than a sudden gust of wind blew up and tore his hat from his head. He quickly reached up to grab it, but it was too late. It went skittering along the promenade.

'Oh!' cried Evelyn.

'I'll get it!' said Billy.

'I bet I get it first!' yelled Peter.

The two boys chased up the promenade after the retreating fedora, Edward racing along in their wake. Billy surged out ahead of the others and all but threw himself on top of it. His friends immediately gave up the chase.

Scrambling back to his feet, Billy trotted back to the man with the cane, wiping sand off the brim with one elbow.

Billy handed him the hat and the man nodded his thanks, reached into his pocket and then handed something over to him. Billy stared down into his palm, there was another brief exchange between them, and then the man turned and limped away.

When Billy returned to the group, he held out a shiny new sixpence. 'Look what he gave me!' he said.

'Gosh!' said Peter. 'You lucky devil!'

'Peter!'

'Sorry, Mum.'

Billy looked at the sixpence. 'Can we buy a dog for a tanner?' he asked Beryl.

'I think they cost a bit more than that,' she replied.

'All right,' he said, glancing from Peter to Edward. 'I'll split it with you two, then. We can have tuppence each.'

Jeannie frowned. 'What about me?' she whined.

Evelyn gave her a squeeze. 'Here you are, poppet. *I'll* give you tuppence.'

It was late afternoon by the time they decided to make their way back home. They'd gone as far as the harbour, where the fishing boats were docked side by side, then on past a jumble of large nets which were strewn across poles beside the quay, drying slowly in the salty air. It had been a lovely day, but the walk and the sea air had eventually tired them out.

'Come on, you four!' said Beryl, watching the children drag their heels up the path behind her. 'I think it'll be an early night for some, don't you, Evelyn?'

'Yes,' Evelyn replied. 'Including me!'

The weekend went all too quickly, and almost before they knew it, Monday morning dawned grey and chilly. Breakfast that day was a solemn affair, because Evelyn was going back to London and both she and Peter knew they would have to go through the agony of saying goodbye all over again.

After breakfast, they all set out for school, with the boys taking turns to carry Evelyn's case for her. Outside the school gate, Evelyn finally bade Peter a tearful farewell.

'Look after yourself, love,' she choked. 'I'll come and see you again as soon as I'm able.'

Not trusting himself to speak, Peter only nodded.

It was almost impossible for her to let him go, but she'd known it would be that way. Beryl, standing with the others a few feet away, swallowed hard to keep her own emotions in check.

'You be a good boy for Mrs Price,' whispered Evelyn.

'Yes, Mum,' said Peter, his bottom lip trembling.

At last Beryl could stand it no more. Stepping forward, she said thickly, 'Evelyn, I've been thinking. Why don't you come and stay here with us until all this war business dies down? You'd be more than welcome.'

Peter's tearful eyes saucered. 'Oh, Mum!' he cried. 'That'd be great! Then Dad could come and see us *both* next time he gets home!'

Evelyn looked uncomfortable. 'I'd only be

a burden,' she protested. 'What with the baby coming and everything.'

'That's all the more reason you *should* stay,' argued Beryl. 'You'll need help sooner or later, and I'll be on call night and day!'

Evelyn felt Peter's eyes on her, willing her to say yes.

'At least *think* about it,' said Beryl. 'That room upstairs'll only stand empty.'

'Well, Tom *did* say he wanted me to move out for the duration,' she murmured. Then, reaching a decision, she said more firmly, 'All right, Beryl. Thank you.'

'Oh, Mum!'

'I'll have to go back first, mind,' Evelyn continued as she gave Peter one more hug. 'There'll be things to sort out and settle.'

But Peter didn't mind about that. All that mattered was that his mother was going to come here and live with him.

'So long as you're sure it's all right with you,' Evelyn told Beryl after blowing her nose and drying her eyes.

'Of course it is,' Beryl assured her, taking her by one arm. 'Look, you just leave all your things at the cottage, do whatever you've got to do back home and then hurry back here.'

Evelyn nodded. 'I'll do that,' she husked. 'I'll be back before you know it.'

Evelyn caught the ten o'clock train back to

London. Beryl waved her off, then walked into the village, already looking forward to the other woman's return.

Cheeky Joe's van was parked in its usual spot beside the village green.

''Morning, Joe,' she called.

Joe was sorting through a few bits and pieces in the back of the van, but turned at the sound of her cheery greeting.

''Mornin' Mrs Price. And how are *you* today?'

'Very well, thanks. And yourself?'

He jumped down from the van to stand beside her. 'Not so bad, you know. Not sure how much longer I'll be trading, though.'

Beryl frowned. 'Things aren't that bad, are they?'

'You'd be surprised,' he replied. 'I'm already starting to notice how hard it is to get hold of some of my staples, and now I hear they plan to start rationing petrol before much longer.' He shrugged. 'Anyway, that's enough of my troubles. What can I do you for, me darlin'?'

'Do you have any lemon-coloured knitting wool?'

'I'll be very surprised if I haven't,' he replied. 'Let's have a look.'

As he climbed back into the van Beryl called, 'Some lemon-coloured buttons as well, while you're there.'

'Right-o,' said Joe. He dragged a large box

to the open doors. 'Here, have a rummage in here while I get the buttons.'

Beryl made her choice, and set several balls of wool to one side.

'Someone's going to be busy,' Joe observed as he came back.

'I've got someone coming to stay for a while,' Beryl explained. 'And she's expecting, so I thought I'd make her a few bits. You know, in advance.'

Joe smiled. 'That'll be nice,' he said. 'A bit of company, like.' He studied her for a moment, then said, 'You're looking very well, I must say, Mrs Price.'

'I *feel* well.'

'I'm glad to hear it. Good news like that, you know, it perks a man up.'

Beryl paid for the goods. 'I do hope you don't have to give the shop up, Joe. Let's just hope this war ends as quickly as it started, eh?'

'Well, my love,' he said with a heartfelt sigh, 'we can always hope.'

Beryl was just approaching the cottage when she spotted a man limping away from her front door, cane in hand. She recognized him immediately as the man whose hat Billy had saved during their visit to Fenby.

He glanced up as she drew nearer, stopped with one hand on the crooked gate and immediately doffed his fedora, revealing a head of thick, sideswept brown hair. 'Uh, good morning, ma'am,' he said, his voice strong but soft, his tone subservient. 'I just tried knocking, but there was no-one home.'

'Well, I'm back now,' Beryl replied cautiously. 'Can I help you?'

He was much younger than she had first imagined, certainly not yet forty, but his unfashionable beard, which he wore neatly clipped, aged him. He was tall and lean, almost hungry-looking, with clear skin, brown eyes, a straight nose and a sad mouth.

Drawing down a deep breath he said, 'I'm looking for work, and I couldn't help noticing that you've got an orchard out back that looks like it could stand a bit of tidying up.'

'Oh,' said Beryl, surprised.

'Don't let my gammy leg fool you,' he said with a self-conscious smile. 'I can put my hand to most things. You know, gardening, farming, carpentry, painting ... anything, really.'

She shrugged uncomfortably. 'I suppose you could always ask in the village,' she suggested. 'There might be someone who needs a few odd jobs doing there.'

'You're not interested in getting the orchard back up and running, then?' he asked. 'I don't mean to be so pushy, but I really *do* need the work.'

'I'm sorry,' she replied. 'The orchard was more my husband's than mine. In fact, I've been thinking of selling the land.'

'Well, there you go, then!' he said, brightening a little. 'I could get it up and running for you in no time, make it a better prospect!' Almost desperately he continued, 'You're in a good position at the moment, you know, what with all this talk of rationing, and the Government looking to the likes of yourself to feed the nation.'

Beryl hadn't looked at it that way before, and again she heard Evelyn saying, *Someone's trying to tell you something...*

'It's something I'd have to think about,' she said at last. 'I mean, it's not a decision I could make alone. I'd have to talk it over with–'

The man nodded. 'Of course,' he said. 'I understand. You'd need to discuss it with your husband first.'

Beryl was about to correct him, but suddenly decided to say nothing. She felt sorry for him. He seemed genuine and desperate to be helpful and to make something of himself. But she reminded herself that he was still a stranger, and yet, oddly enough, not like a stranger at all.

The man placed the hat back on his head and gave her a respectful nod. 'Well, it's been a pleasure meeting you, Mrs, uh...'

'Price,' she said.

'My name's Gordon, Mrs Price,' he replied. 'Harry Gordon. And if you *do* decide to do something with your orchard ... well, I

212

daresay I'll be around.'

He turned and limped off toward the village.

On the way home from school that afternoon, Billy kicked a stone in Peter's direction and said, 'I wish we had a football.'

Beryl had met Edward, Peter and Jeannie from school, and then all four had gone to collect Billy from the village hall, where Miss Ferguson's class now held its lessons.

'What happened to your football, Edward?' Beryl asked.

'It went flat, and I couldn't find Dad's foot pump to blow it up again,' he answered.

'Have a look in the shed,' Beryl suggested. 'It wasn't upstairs with his tools, so it's probably out there.'

Edward didn't fancy going into the old shed. It was full of cobwebs. But Billy shared no such reluctance.

'I'll help you!' he volunteered.

When they got home, Billy, Peter and Edward dragged the shed door open and peered inside. The hinges had rusted, the door had dropped and they had to put up quite a struggle just to open it a crack. Billy, being somewhat shorter and slighter than his companions, slipped through the narrow opening and began to search for the foot pump.

The gloomy shed was crammed with different lengths and thicknesses of wood, an assortment of garden tools, empty flower-pots and goodness knew what else.

'Cor, a bike!' called Billy.

'That'll be my dad's,' replied Edward. 'Look on the bench, Billy. If the pump's anywhere, it'll be on there.'

'I don't even know what a foot pump looks like!' Billy confessed.

Peter rolled his eyes. '*Now* he tells us!'

'It looks a bit like a policeman's truncheon,' Edward said helpfully.

'Is this it?' asked Billy, thrusting the foot pump through the gap for their inspection.

'That's it!'

It wasn't long before Edward was once again in possession of a perfectly good football. 'Come on,' he said. 'We'll go play down by the abbey.'

The boys were enjoying their kick-about when Billy glanced up and spotted the man in the fedora watching them from the stile. He had no idea how long the man had been there.

'Hello, lads,' he called. 'Having fun?'

'Yeah,' said Billy.

'Want to play?' asked Edward.

Harry Gordon glanced down at his stiff leg. 'I'd love to, if it wasn't for this.'

Going a little closer, Peter said, 'Is it made of wood?'

Harry laughed. 'No, it's real enough. It just doesn't work the way it used to.'

'How did you hurt it?'

'I had an accident a few years ago. A crash.'

'Did you break it?' Billy wanted to know.

'Yes. The leg *and* my hip.' He smiled suddenly. 'You spent that sixpence yet, lad?' he asked.

'We had tuppence each,' said Billy. 'We bought sweets.'

Harry nodded. 'I'd have done the same at your age.'

There followed a long, uncomfortable silence, after which Harry said, 'Well, I suppose I'd better let you get on with your game, then, otherwise you'll have to go into extra time.'

'All right,' said Peter. ''Bye.'

Harry turned and limped off down the lane.

Billy scowled after him. 'He gives me the creeps,' he muttered.

'I thought he was quite friendly,' said Peter.

'Maybe that's what he *wanted* you to think,' Billy said darkly. 'For all we know, he could be a German spy.'

Edward's mouth dropped open. 'Do you think so?'

Billy shrugged. 'I wouldn't be surprised.'

All three turned to watch the figure shuffling away. A German spy! It was certainly something to think about.

Chapter Nineteen

The Hired Man

On Thursday morning, Beryl received a letter from Evelyn. She'd written to give Tom her new address at Holly Cottage, had left it as a forwarding address with her next-door neighbour, had packed everything she could comfortably carry and was planning to catch the 11:40 train from Liverpool Street Station on Saturday. Peter was overjoyed at the news.

Beryl and the children were at Little Asham station to meet her on Saturday afternoon. When the train rolled in, Peter and the other boys rushed to help her with her luggage, and there were hugs all round.

'How on earth did you manage to carry all this?' asked Beryl.

'I haven't brought too much, have I?' Evelyn countered worriedly.

'Of course not! I just wondered how you did it!'

'I was lucky. I got a lift to the station from our coalman, and he helped me right onto the train.'

'Do you mean Sam, Mum?' asked Peter.

'Yes. He's a lovely feller, do anything for anyone. He was making a couple of deliveries around Liverpool Street, so I hopped on.'

They walked slowly back to the cottage, the boys struggling manfully with the cases, and before long the two women were sitting at the kitchen table and the children went out to play.

'Oh, it's lovely to be back,' Evelyn grinned.

'And it's lovely to *have* you back,' Beryl replied.

After a while the conversation turned to Harry Gordon, and how he'd been around, looking for work.

'Do you think he'll be back?' asked Evelyn.

'I don't know. I *hope* so. I couldn't help feeling sorry for him, somehow.'

Evelyn sipped her tea. 'And he had a point,' she added. 'About the orchard, I mean. If things go the way they say they will, it won't be long before the country's crying out for fruit and veg suppliers.'

'We'll see if he shows his face again, then,' decided Beryl. 'I won't feel quite so intimidated if you're here as well!'

The children had gone as far as the abbey, where they lazed on the rocky outcrop.

The place didn't seem at all frightening on that sunny but chilly afternoon, and all thought of ghosts had long-since been dispelled. Even Jeannie was happy to explore the ruins on her own, while the boys chatted.

The sound of an aircraft caught their attention once more, and they all looked skyward, shielding their eyes from the bright sunlight. Its undercarriage was down as it came in low. In fact, it was so low that it seemed they might almost be able to see the pilot. Then the plane disappeared with a roar into the field beyond the farmland, and all was silent again except for the whirr of a tractor engine from the field alongside the abbey, and the clamour of hundreds of sea-gulls descending on the tilled earth in its wake.

Peter sat up suddenly and slid down off the stone slab. 'Come on, let's play hide and seek!'

'Who's going to find who?' asked Billy.

'I'll seek!' said Edward, and clapping his hands over his eyes he called, 'Right. I'll give you to the count of ten! One ... two...'

He heard the sound of disappearing foot-steps, as the other boys sought cover.

At last he yelled, *'Ten! Coming, ready or not!'*

He opened his eyes, squinting against the sudden brightness, then set off in search of his quarry. Billy and Peter were nowhere to be found at the back of the ruins, so he stealthily worked his way around to the front, catching a glimpse of Jeannie walking towards the stile with some wild flowers clutched in her hand.

He came to a spot where there were several good hiding places among the fallen columns, and that was where he found Peter, crouched in the tall grass beside the steps. Peter let out a loud shriek when Edward tapped him lightly on the head.

'Got you!' he cried. 'Now come on, let's find Billy!'

By this time Jeannie had perched herself on the stile, the flowers in one hand, her baby doll asleep in the other. She was singing softly to herself when she heard someone coming down the lane from the direction of Fenby.

Looking round, she saw that it was the man with the bad leg. He was whistling a familiar tune, entirely unaware of her presence until he drew almost level with her.

'You're whistling my song!' Jeannie cried, her little face beaming.

The man stopped, spun and then looked at her for a long, almost uncomfortable moment before finally relaxing and returning her smile with a slow, vaguely sad one of his own. 'Am I really?' he said at last, and then, clearing his throat, he sang softly, "'I dream of Jeannie with the light brown hair…'"

'That's *me!*' Jeannie said excitedly. '*I'm* Jeannie and *I've* got light brown hair!' She pulled at the wavy locks behind her ears, trying not to drop the flowers.

They could hear the boys laughing beyond the hedge, then Billy's voice calling her name.

'That's my brother,' she explained. 'They've been playing hide and seek.'

'Well, you'd better tell him where you are,' said Harry.

Jeannie got to her feet and called back, 'I'm *here!*'

The boys came running, but pulled up sharp when they saw whom she was with.

Billy scowled at her. 'You mustn't talk to strangers,' he said.

'He's not a stranger,' she replied. 'We saw him at the seaside!'

'No, the lad's right,' said Harry. 'You can't be too careful these days, Jeannie. But my name's Harry. Harry Gordon. So now we're not strangers anymore, are we?'

'Harry was *singing!*' said Jeannie.

Harry shrugged. 'Well, if you could *call* it that.' He gestured towards the abbey. 'Nice spot, this,' he murmured almost to himself. 'Quiet. A man can do his thinking here, eh?'

He stared at Billy but received no response.

With a shrug he bade them farewell, and as he limped away, Jeannie called, 'I hope I see you again!'

'I hope so, too!' called Harry.

Billy was furious. 'Jeannie,' he snapped, 'That was naughty!'

But the little girl couldn't see any harm in what she'd done. 'No it wasn't!' she retorted. With a scowl, she jumped off the stile into the lane and started marching back toward the cottage.

The three boys followed behind her, with Billy eventually pushing on ahead. When he drew level with her he said, 'I'm goin' to tell Mrs Price about *you.*' And with that, he ran off.

Jeannie stood in the lane until Edward and Peter came up beside her. Her bottom lip was trembling.

By the time the three of them reached home, Billy had told Beryl everything. But as much as she appreciated his obvious concern, she couldn't help but feel sorry for Jeannie when she finally came through the door, her face wet with tears, the wilting flowers till clutched in one hand.

'All right,' she said. 'No harm done. Billy, you're quite right. It *is* naughty to talk to strangers. But I know the man you mean. I spoke to him myself last Monday. He seems like a very nice gentleman.'

'We think he's a German spy!' blurted Peter.

'I hardly think so,' said Beryl. 'Just what did he do to you, poppet?'

Jeannie said, 'He sung to me. He sung my song.'

'Well, he doesn't sound much like a German spy to me,' said Beryl. 'Now, go and wash your hands, the lot of you. Tea's almost ready.'

As the children filed out, Evelyn said, 'So, he's still around, then?'

'Yes. And if I see him, I might ask him if he's still interested in working in the orchard.'

'Good for you!'

But as it turned out, they didn't see Harry Gordon again until the following Thursday afternoon, when Evelyn was putting washing through a wringer in the back garden and Beryl was sweeping the front path. As he went limping by, he touched the brim of his hat and said, 'Good afternoon, Mrs Price.'

Engrossed in her work, Beryl jumped in surprise at the unexpected greeting. 'Oh!'

'I'm sorry,' he said. 'I didn't mean to startle you.'

Hearing the cry, Evelyn hurried around the side of the house. Seeing her, Harry immediately touched the brim of his hat.

'Evelyn, this is uh, Harry Gordon. Harry, this is my friend, Evelyn. Evelyn Murray.'

'I believe we met briefly a few weeks ago, in Fenby,' said Evelyn.

'That's right. You were having a picnic, weren't you?'

'Well, jam and sand sandwiches, yes.'

'And one of your lads saved my hat.'

Chancing a brief glance at Evelyn, Beryl said, 'Did you have any luck finding work after all, uh, Harry?'

''Fraid not. Times are hard all over.'

'Then you could probably use a cup of tea.'

He looked pleasantly surprised by the invitation. 'I've never been known to *refuse* one.'

'We, ah, might also have a proposition for you,' Beryl said, dry-mouthed.

Over the next half hour, she explained her situation and offered Harry the full run of the orchard in exchange for a percentage of the takings, plus a hearty meal at the end of each day.

'Well, I don't quite know what to say,' he replied. During the course of the conversation, they'd found out that he'd moved up from London about a month earlier, that he was a widower and was living in a rented room in Fenby. He didn't have much in the way of family, but was keen to do almost anything if it meant he could contribute to the war effort and earn himself an honest living.

'I don't expect you to make up your mind right this minute,' said Beryl. 'But we'll certainly need a helping hand if we're to restore the orchard.'

'Oh, I don't have to think about it,' he replied. 'I'd be proud to take the job, and you won't be sorry, either.'

Beryl raised her cup. 'It's settled, then.'

He rose from the table and retrieved his hat and cane. 'If you like, I'll take a quick wander around now. You know, see what needs doing first.'

Beryl also got to her feet. 'You'll find all the tools you need in the shed – if you can get the door open wide enough! They haven't been used for a couple of years, but I think you'll find everything you're likely to need.'

'And I'm sure the boys will be only too happy to give you a hand,' Evelyn added.

Once Harry had disappeared, Beryl raised her eyebrows and whispered, 'I hope I've done the right thing.'

'Of course you have! Anyway, if it doesn't work out, you'll just have to let him go,' Evelyn counseled. 'He seems a decent sort, I must say. Very polite.'

'Yes,' Beryl murmured. 'But I'm sure I've seen him somewhere before. I just can't place where, though.'

The grandmother clock chimed three.

'Good grief!' said Beryl. 'The children'll be home in a minute! Where has the day gone?'

The children had just gone out to play when Edward noticed a figure wandering around the orchard. He stopped and peered through some winter-stripped bushes to get a better look.

Realising that something was amiss, the others hurriedly joined him. 'What is it?' whispered Peter.

'Someone's in the orchard!' breathed Edward.

Indeed there was. A man was wandering between the trees, stopping every now and then to feel the bark or examine the fruit itself.

Almost immediately Billy said, 'It's him! The spy!'

'Harry?' asked Jeannie.

'We'd better tell Mum!' Edward said determinedly.

Beryl was picking vegetables for their dinner when the children found her.

'Mum!' Edward said urgently. 'That man's in the orchard!'

'The German spy!' said Billy.

'You know,' said Peter in a state of high excitement. 'The one who doesn't have a wooden leg!'

Beryl glanced up. 'Yes,' she said. 'I know he's in the orchard.'

'But ... what's he doing there?'

'He's our new hired man,' explained Beryl.

She pushed to her feet and walked back toward the cottage, carrying her vegetable-filled basket with her. By coincidence, Harry had also been heading for the back door, and they met on the path to the scullery. The boys came to an abrupt halt and almost, but not quite, tried to hide behind Beryl.

'You've already met Harry,' said Beryl. 'Well, from now on, he's going to help us in the orchard.'

'Hello, kids,' said Harry.

Jeannie, not sharing the boy's misgivings, offered Harry a shy wave. He wiggled his fingers back at her.

'Harry's a Londoner, just like us,' called Evelyn, who had been peeling potatoes at the sink.

Harry looked at Beryl. 'Well, I've had a good look round, Mrs Price,' he said. 'And I don't see any problems. You grow Golden Knobs, don't you?'

Beryl was impressed. 'Well, you certainly know your apples.'

'I know the Golden Knob,' he said. 'Sweet and sharp, just how an apple *should* be. Anyway, I'll be back early tomorrow and make a start on clearing some of the brambles, if that's all right?'

Beryl nodded. 'You know where everything is, so just help yourself. We'll have the kettle boiling.'

Harry nodded. 'Well, good afternoon, and thank you once again.' He turned to the children. 'See you tomorrow.'

Everyone bade Harry goodbye, except Billy, who watched him go with a scowl.

'I like Harry!' Jeannie announced.

'Well *I* don't!' murmured Billy.

'Billy!' said Beryl.

'What's wrong with him, love?' asked Evelyn, coming outside to join them. 'Still think he's a German in disguise?'

Billy shrugged. 'How do we know he's *not?*' he replied.

The following morning, Peter was woken by a persistent squeaking. He sat up and dry-washed his sleepy face. The sound seemed to be coming from the garden.

Seeing that Edward was already awake, he asked, 'What's that noise?'

It was only just getting light, and Beryl hadn't yet called them to get ready for school.

'It's Harry!' said Jeannie, stretching and pulling herself out of her tangled bed-clothes. Doll in hand, as always, she stepped over Peter, then Billy, then pulled back the curtain and peered out into the chilly dawn.

'What's he doing?' asked Edward, kneeling on his pillow to get a better look.

Billy was also awake, but at the mention of Harry's name, he buried his head deeper beneath the covers.

'He's pushing a wheelbarrow into the orchard,' said Jeannie. She tapped on the window to attract the man's attention, and squealed when he turned and looked up then threw her a cheery wave before disappearing through the arch in the hedge.

Just then the bedroom door opened and Beryl came in wearing a thick, burgundy dressing-down. 'My, you *are* up early this morning!'

'Harry *woke* us up,' Billy complained from beneath the bedclothes.

Jeannie hurried toward Beryl for what had now become her usual good-morning kiss. She stumbled on Peter's legs and fell across her brother. The accident did nothing to improve his mood.

'Oi!' he growled. 'Watch it!'

'Harry's here!' Jeannie said, climbing back to her feet.

Beryl pulled her dressing-gown more tightly around her. 'He *is* early! I'd better get the kettle going.'

Downstairs, Beryl told Jeannie to ask Harry if he'd like some breakfast. The little girl, who by now was washed and dressed, was only too happy to oblige.

Harry was just adding to an ever-growing pile of brambles when Jeannie raced up.

'Hello, little 'un,' he greeted warmly. 'You're an early bird this morning.'

'I saw you from the window,' Jeannie said, shyly.

'I know. I suppose my squeaky wheel woke you up, didn't it? I'll have to oil it.'

Jeannie suddenly remembered why she

was there. 'Mu – uh, Mrs Price said would you like some porridge?'

Harry frowned. 'What did you nearly call her, then?'

'Nothing.'

'Come on, out with it.'

Jeannie shrugged and peered off into the misty distance. 'Mum,' she said softly.

'But she's not your mum, is she?'

'No,' said Jeannie. 'But I wish she *was.*'

He nodded thoughtfully. 'She's a lovely woman, all right. Anyway, you tell Mrs Price it was very kind of her to ask, but I'm fine just now. All right?'

Jeannie nodded. 'We're going to school in a while, and I'm going to shout goodbye to you through the hedge!'

He grinned down at her. 'I'll listen out for that, then, and shout goodbye back to you. And maybe later on you can tell me what you learned today, eh?'

Jeannie thought that was an excellent idea.

The boys had already taken their places at the kitchen table when she raced back into the house. It was still quite early, and everyone seemed in a happy mood. After all, it was Friday, and Friday meant no school for two whole days.

Billy was more subdued than usual, however. He toyed with his breakfast in near-silence and seemed unwilling to join in with the idle chatter of the others.

'You're very quiet this morning,' Evelyn noted as she sat down next to him. 'Are you feeling all right?'

Billy just nodded.

'Cat got your tongue?' she teased.

'We haven't got a cat,' growled Billy.

'Oh dear,' she said. 'You *are* an old grump this morning.'

'Maybe we can all do something nice tomorrow,' Beryl suggested.

'Can we go to the seaside again?' Jeannie asked excitedly. 'We might see Harry there!'

Billy gave his sister a glare. 'You can see Harry any day of the *week,* now,' he muttered.

'All right, grouchy,' said Beryl. 'Turn that frown upside-down – or else!'

Edward and Peter cleaned their bowls and then went to collect their gas masks from the hook on the scullery wall. Billy pushed his bowl away from him and stood up. He'd hardly touched his breakfast.

'Are you sure you're feeling all right?' asked Evelyn.

He shrugged. 'Not really,' he replied.

Evelyn placed the back of her hand against his forehead. 'You *are* a bit hot, I must say.' She glanced at Beryl for guidance.

'Perhaps you ought to stay home today,' Beryl suggested, helping Jeannie on with her coat. She wasn't entirely sure that Billy was unwell, but she was wiling to give him the benefit of the doubt, just this once. 'Go on, you three. Off you go!'

'What about Billy?' asked Peter.

'Billy's not feeling well, so make sure you tell Miss Ferguson I'm keeping him home today.'

While Beryl ushered the children towards the front door, Evelyn gathered up the breakfast things and poured hot water into an enamel bowl. 'Do you want to go back to bed?' she asked.

Billy considered the question for a moment, then nodded.

'I'll tell you what,' said Evelyn. 'Go and make yourself comfortable in Edward's bed. I'm sure he won't mind.'

Against his will, Billy began to feel better at the prospect of having a day off school. He hadn't lied to Mrs Price, either. He didn't feel ill, exactly, but neither did he feel quite *right*. With a nod he climbed the stairs to the bedroom, changed back into his pyjamas and jumped into Edward's bed.

At once he felt warm and safe and cosy. What a luxury this was, after weeks of sleeping on the floor! But try as he might, he just couldn't go off to sleep. He almost managed it once, but the persistent squeak of the old wheelbarrow woke him up again with a start.

He threw back the covers and knelt up in bed so that he could peer out into the garden beyond. He saw Harry busily pulling overgrown brambles from a hedge and piling them into the wheelbarrow.

'Not asleep yet?'

Billy turned as Evelyn entered the room, carrying a cup of warm milk and a few biscuits.

He shrugged. 'I can't go off. That wheelbarrow keeps disturbing me.'

'Does it, indeed? Can I get you a book to read, then?'

Billy screwed up his nose and shook his head. 'Can I come downstairs?'

''Course you can. You can sit at the kitchen table and do some drawing, if you like.'

He nodded, pushed back the sheets and reached for his clothes.

Suddenly there came the sound of a lorry pulling up outside. 'What on earth was that?' asked Evelyn.

She went downstairs to find out, and discovered Beryl watching two men lifting a series of shiny corrugated steel panels off the back of a truck and carrying them along the side of the house to the back garden. She recognised them immediately.

'That's an Anderson shelter, isn't it?'

'Well, it *will* be, once we put it all together,' replied Beryl. 'It cost me seven pounds, but if worse comes to worst, it'll be money well spent.'

When Billy entered the kitchen a few minutes later, he heard voices coming from the garden. Poking his head out through the back door, he saw that all the panels – some straight, several curved, one with a door aperture cut out of it – had been propped up against one wall, awaiting assembly. Beryl, Evelyn and Harry were studying them.

'Hello, love!' said Beryl, turning when she heard Billy come up behind them. 'Have you come to help?'

'What is it?' asked Billy.

It was Harry who supplied the answer, glancing up from the nuts and bolts spread out on the ground before them. 'It's an air-raid shelter,' he said. Frowning suddenly, he asked, 'No school today, lad?'

'He wasn't feeling very well,' said Beryl.

Harry reached out and tousled his hair. Billy immediately tried to squirm out of his reach. 'I'm sorry to hear that,' said Harry, and he sounded as if he meant it. 'Perhaps when you feel a bit better you can give me a hand here, eh?'

Billy shrugged. The last thing he wanted to do was spend time with a German spy.

'I thought over there would be the best place for it,' Beryl explained, gesturing to a spot at the back of the garden. 'It's far enough away from the house, but not so far that we can't get to it in a hurry.'

'All right,' said Harry. 'I'll fetch a shovel

and start digging. According to the instructions, it has to go down four feet.' Again he looked at Billy. 'Fancy helping me, son?'

Billy shook his head.

'He was going to do some drawing at the kitchen table,' said Evelyn.

Harry shrugged. 'Well, he can do it just as well out here. That way he can keep me company and get plenty of clean country air down his lungs at the same time.'

While Harry went off to find a shovel and start measuring out the trench he needed to dig, Beryl set a kitchen chair just outside the scullery door and Billy sat down with pencil and paper and started to draw.

By lunchtime, he'd produced an impressive collection of drawings, and Harry, now flushed and sweating, had more or less completed the trench. When Beryl came out with tea and sandwiches for them, she noticed a sketch Billy had made of Harry at work, and paused to admire it.

'Billy!' she said in surprise. 'I didn't realise you were so talented. Why don't you show Harry what you've done?'

'Maybe when it's finished,' Billy hedged.

'Well, what else have you drawn?' she asked with interest.

Billy showed her a drawing of Holly Cottage. 'You can have that one, if you like,' he mumbled self-consciously.

'Thank you. That'll go in pride of place,'

she said, taking it. 'I tell you what. I'll find you a box later, and you can keep all your drawings in it.'

'Thanks,' he replied, but as soon as she was gone he slipped the drawing of Harry to the bottom of the pile.

Chapter Twenty

Revelation and Denial

By late afternoon the shelter had been erected. Towards the end, Beryl and Billy had lent a hand. For obvious reasons, Evelyn was excused duty.

'You'll not be doing any heavy work in *your* condition, my girl!' Beryl had said, and that was that.

As reluctant as he was to have anything to do with Harry, Billy became increasingly fascinated as the shelter began to take shape, and was soon handing out nuts, bolts and tools as and when they were needed.

The shelter stood six feet high, a little more than six feet long and four and a half feet wide. It was built from six curved panels that joined to form the roof, three straight panels to either side, which were the walls, a single panel for the back wall and another, the one with the door aperture, for the front.

Harry added two steps that led down into the shelter, and then lay three flagstones as a rough and ready floor. Finally, he found a spade for Billy and together they shovelled earth around its three closed sides and packed it tight.

'There,' said Harry at last, wiping a sleeve across his glistening brow. 'It's done.' And without warning he stuck out his right hand and said, 'Put it there, partner. I couldn't have done it without you.'

Billy stared at his hand for a long moment before finally reaching out to shake it.

'Can I have a look inside?' asked Beryl.

''Course you can.'

'We'll have to think about exactly what we'll need down here,' Beryl murmured as she descended into the gloomy shelter and Harry and Billy followed her.

'We'll need a light, won't we?' said Billy.

'Yes. And a little table and maybe a few chairs.'

Suddenly there came a chorus of excited voices from outside, and a moment later three inquisitive faces peered through the narrow doorway.

'Cor!' breathed Peter. 'It's a secret den!'

Evelyn, who had met the children from school, came down the steps to join them. 'What will it be like when we're all in there?'

she asked.

There was only one way to find out.

'There's not much room, is there?' said Edward.

'Never mind,' said Beryl. 'By the time I'm finished, it'll be a regular home from home!'

Between them, the children carried out all the essentials Beryl thought they would need – cushions, blankets, candles, matches and more. Beryl sorted out three old chairs and some stools for the children, plus an old Marconiphone 262 wireless set.

Three weeks were to pass, however, before they got the chance to put the shelter to the test.

It was a Sunday morning in November, the children were dressing for church and the grandmother clock had just chimed nine o'clock. Beryl called up the stairs to tell everyone to hurry up, while Evelyn struggled in vain to button her coat.

'I'll have to leave it open, I think,' she decided at length, glancing at herself in the hall mirror. 'It's not going to fit for much longer, anyway.'

Suddenly, from the direction of the village, came a low, unfamiliar whining sound that slowly but steadily rose in volume.

For a moment then time stood still, for the villagers had been told that the siren would only ever be used in the event of an air raid. Then the spell broke and the two women called urgently to the children, who came downstairs at a run, more excited than scared.

'*Don't run!*' called Beryl.

She grasped Jeannie's hand and together with Evelyn and the three boys, hurried through to the kitchen. After making sure everyone had their gas mask, they went out into the cool, misty garden.

They had just reached the shelter when a new sound drifted through the air – the grumbling snarl of aeroplane engines.

It froze them in their tracks, and as one they turned their eyes skyward.

Edward saw it first. '*There!*'

As they watched, Beryl and Evelyn fearing the worst, the black dot grew in size, and one by one they realized that something was wrong with the aircraft. It seemed to be wobbling, then straightening out, its wings constantly dipping, then levelling, then dipping again.

As the dot slowly took on definition, the sound of its engines grew louder. To Edward's keen ear the sound was strangely uneven. He squinted up at the machine, which seemed to be enormous, even from this distance. Two black, wing-mounted propellers, with their tips painted bright yellow, were whirring furiously to either side of a large Perspex dome. But the starboard one seemed to be spinning at a slower rate – so slow, in fact, that they could clearly make out each of its three blades.

'What is it, Edward?' asked Billy. 'A Wellington, I bet.'

Jeannie's mouth dropped open. 'A boot?' she asked in astonishment.

'No,' said Billy. 'A bomber. The plane that's goin' to teach old Adolf a lesson!'

'It's not a Wellington,' murmured Edward.

The plane was so close now that they could make out its green and grey camouflage markings. And it was still rising and falling, dipping and tilting, the engines alternately growling then purring, growling then purring.

A second later the engines cut out altogether. The silence was ominous, awful, and it was a relief when they caught again.

'It's a Beaufort,' Edward half-whispered. Then, louder, 'A Bristol Beaufort! And it's in trouble!'

That much was now clear to all of them. They could even see the pilot and co-pilot at the controls, the machine was that low. And, as it came closer, its vast shadow skittering across the ground beneath it, the roar of its one good engine hammering at their eardrums, the wheels suddenly came down from their bays in its wings.

'He's in *real* trouble!' Edward said urgently, unable to tear his eyes away from the aircraft.

Nearer it came, the machine dropping, lifting, dropping again all the while. And then, finally, inevitably, the starboard engine gave out once and for all, and the Beaufort lurched.

'It's going to crash!' bellowed Edward.

Everyone held their breath, rooted to the spot by the awful certainty that the plane was going to come down, and they could only watch and pray as it passed over them, almost skimming the trees, until it was lost behind them.

Hearts in mouths they waited, expecting to hear an almighty crash as the plane came down, and see the huge black cloud of exploding petrol tanks rising up into the otherwise peaceful Norfolk sky.

But incredibly, nothing happened.

They suddenly realised that the siren was no longer whining, that Mr King, the ARP warden, must have realised it was just a false alarm.

Peter licked his dry lips. 'Maybe he wasn't in trouble after all?' he hazarded.

Edward nodded slowly. 'Let's hope so.'

But the plane *had* been in trouble, as they heard later. Engine failure had forced the pilot and his crew, who had been on a test flight to familiarise themselves with the aircraft, to make an emergency landing in a field just beyond the abbey. It had been rough – one of the wheels had caught in the uneven ground and been torn off. The bomber had slid along on its vast underbelly, a petrol tank rupturing, spilling flammable liquid everywhere.

The four-man crew had been lucky to get out alive. And they might not have, had it not been for the first man on the scene, who dragged them to safety.

After school the following day, the children made their way up to the abbey in hope that they might catch a glimpse of the wreckage. They climbed on to the highest accessible part of the ruins, but still couldn't see beyond the high bushes that bordered the field.

Impetuous as ever, Billy ran to the far corner, where the bushes were thinned. He managed to squeeze through a small hole, scratching his arms as he did so, but the sight that met his eyes on the far side was well worth the discomfort.

''Ere, come an' see this!' he called back to the others.

Peter slipped through the gap and held the branches back for Jeannie, then Edward, to clamber through behind him.

'Gosh!'

Twisted wreckage was strewn across the field, but the actual fuselage of the Beaufort was still intact. The bomber lay in the middle of the field, scorched in places, like some huge, sleeping dragonfly. It had gouged a tremendous scar out of the earth behind it.

All at once a young soldier appeared as if from out of nowhere. 'And just what do you think *you're* doing?' he snapped.

The children jumped and shuffled guiltily for a moment, until Billy said, 'Oh, come on, mate. We only want to take a look.'

'Well, you *can't*,' said the soldier. 'This is Ministry of Defence property, see, and that's all there is to it.'

One look at the soldier's face convinced them that he meant what he said, so with a reluctant final glance at the wreckage, they turned and scrambled back through the hedge.

The four children walked slowly back to the abbey and sat down on the steps.

'I've got an idea!' said Billy. 'Why don't we make our own plane, usin' that one as our model?'

Peter frowned. 'How are we going to remember what it looks like? They won't let us back in the field.'

'Easy!' grinned Billy. 'I'll draw it!'

'Draw it?' echoed Edward.

Billy nodded. 'I'll run back to the cottage and get some paper and a pencil,' he said, jumping to his feet. 'You two can be lookouts, while I crawl through the bush again and draw it!'

Jeannie couldn't really see what all the fuss was about. 'I'm going back to the cottage as well,' she said.

Edward and Peter took up their places by the hole in the hedge and waited as patiently as they could for Billy to return. When he finally came racing back, Edward gestured that he should slow down and make less noise. Billy immediately threw himself down onto his tummy and crawled the rest of the way.

'The guard's on the other side of the bush,' Edward said in a whisper as Billy snaked up beside them. 'You'll have to wait until he walks back the other way before you can go through!'

'He seems to walk so far one way, then turns and comes back,' noted Peter. 'So you'll have to be quick.'

Billy gave the matter some thought. 'I might have to do it bit by bit,' he concluded.

'Right,' said Edward. 'Go through now, while he's got his back to us!'

Billy slipped through the hedge and sprawled out in the grass bordering the field. With the tip of his tongue protruding from the corner of his mouth, he began to draw.

'*Billy!*' Peter whispered urgently. 'He's coming back!'

Billy immediately dived for the hedge, trying to keep his paper from creasing.

'No, wait!' said Edward. 'He's talking to another guard.'

'Go back,' said Peter.

Billy shook his head. 'Well, make your bleedin' minds up,' he hissed.

He returned to his spot and continued sketching.

In all, it took five attempts before Billy finished the sketch. Then he came back through the bushes and proudly held up the product of his labours.

'That's fantastic!' said Peter, studying the fine detail that Billy had added.

'Come on, then,' Edward added excitedly. 'Now we've got our top-secret plan, we can get started!'

They raced back to the cottage.

As they came through the door, they saw Harry sitting at the kitchen table, drinking a cup of tea.

'We've seen the plane!' Edward burst out.

Beryl turned to him from the sink. 'I do hope you weren't doing anything you shouldn't have,' she said.

'Billy's done a fantastic drawing of it!' panted Peter. 'Look!'

He took the piece of paper from Billy and spread it out on the table.

'How did you get so close to it?' Harry asked with a frown.

'Billy had to sneak into the field and draw it while the guards weren't looking,' supplied Edward, admiring the sketch over Harry's shoulder.

'Is that right, lad?' asked Harry.

Billy nodded.

He expected to get told off, but instead Harry said, 'That took pluck. I bet you'd be as cool as a cucumber under fire.'

Billy looked at him. 'You reckon?'

Harry nodded. 'Wouldn't surprise me if you weren't officer material,' he said.

'I said he was good at art, didn't I?' said Beryl. 'Go and fetch your other sketches, Billy.'

Billy mumbled, 'I don't know where they are.'

''Course you do,' said Evelyn. 'They're in that old shoebox Beryl gave you. Go on – chop-chop!'

'Did he *really* do this?' Harry asked once Billy had left the room.

Edward and Peter nodded.

Billy came back a few moments later, dragging his heels. He put a shoebox on the kitchen table and took off the lid. It was crammed with sketches of all shapes and sizes.

Harry took out a handful and studied them one by one. When he came to the sketch Billy had made of him three weeks earlier, he sat as if frozen, studying the drawing for a long, silent moment.

'You're quite an artist, young man,' he said at last.

Billy mumbled a reluctant, 'Thanks,' then put the drawings back in the box.

'We're going to make our own plane from this,' Edward explained, holding Billy's sketch of the Beaufort.

'Well, if you need any help, just ask Harry,' said Evelyn. 'He saw it close up.'

Peter's mouth dropped open. *Really?*

'You could help us with the colours,' said Edward. 'Couldn't he, Billy?'

Billy shrugged. 'I suppose so.'

'Did you see the pilot?' asked Edward.

'*See* him!' laughed Evelyn. 'Harry saved his life!'

'What?'

'Harry's the man of the moment,' Evelyn continued. '*He* was the one who pulled the crew to safety!'

Impressed, Edward and Peter stared at Harry in open admiration. 'Wow! What happened, Harry?' asked Edward.

Harry shrugged. 'Nothing much. I was in the area, saw the plane come down, went to help. Anyone else would've done the same.'

'Gosh!' said Peter. 'You talk about *Billy* having pluck! I bet they'll give you a medal!'

Billy, meanwhile, was trying to look as if he couldn't care less.

'Billy?' asked Evelyn.

He looked up. 'What?'

'Do you still think Harry's a German spy now?' she asked.

The days grew shorter and chillier, but no

246

matter how cold or inclement it became, Harry could always be found toiling in the orchard. He worked wonders, clearing and cultivating the place, and the children helped him pick the last crop for the year.

Beryl and Evelyn stored as much as they could in wooden boxes inside the scullery, where it was cool and dark, and when all the windfalls had been collected, they set about making pickles and chutneys.

One morning, after the children had gone to school, Evelyn was pegging out the washing when she heard the familiar squeak of the wheelbarrow, and Harry came limping up the path towards her. He had become a regular fixture around Holly Cottage, and following the incident with the Beaufort, even Billy had thawed a little towards him.

Harry drew level with Evelyn and set the barrow down. 'Cold one, this morning,' he noted.

'Yes. And it'll be Christmas before we know it.'

He nodded. 'I think I'll start to thin the trees a bit today, now that the fruit's all gone. That way we'll get a better crop next season.'

'You'll stop for a cup of tea first, though?'

He smiled. 'You know me, Evelyn. I'll *always* stop for a cup of tea.'

'You sound just like my Tom,' Evelyn said as they walked back toward the cottage.

'Peter must miss him something dreadful,'

he observed. 'Well, the pair of you, really.'

'It's the longest we've ever been apart,' Evelyn confessed.

They entered the kitchen and Evelyn began to set out the tea-things while Harry peeled off his work-gloves and took a seat at the table. From the hallway came the familiar sound of the postman delivering that day's mail, and from the parlour Beryl called, 'I'll get it!'

'Tea, Beryl?'

'Go on, then.'

'Be nice if the war's over by Christmas,' Evelyn continued. 'I love it here, but I do miss our little house in London. What about you, Harry? Do you think you'll ever go back to the Smoke?'

Harry shrugged. 'There's nothing much there for me anymore.'

'Don't you have any family there?'

'No. We lost touch years ago. Anyway, I quite like it 'round here.'

'Yes, I know what you mean. It's a lovely place for children.'

Before the conversation could go any further, Beryl entered the kitchen. She was walking slowly, still reading the headed letter she'd just taken from an official manila envelope, and her face had drained of colour.

Evelyn said, 'Beryl? Beryl, are you all right, love?'

Beryl looked up. The letter in her hands

shook, and when she dropped it onto the kitchen table, Evelyn's eyes saw the words *Home Office* and feared the worst.

'Oh God,' she breathed, 'what is it?'

'H-Harry,' said Beryl. 'I … I think we need to talk. And … and I think there's something you need to tell us. To tell *all* of us.'

Harry pulled the collar of his reefer jacket up against the increasingly blustery wind. It had been threatening rain all day, and he wanted to get as much work done as possible before it came. But if the dark clouds overhead were any indicator, there wasn't going to be much chance of that.

The wind whipped up the brittle leaves and sent them capering across the orchard floor as he collected up the tools he'd been using and started over to the shed.

He was halfway there when he heard Jeannie's voice from the lane, and the sounds the boys made playing kick-about. The day had passed with agonizing slowness, but at last the moment he'd been dreading was at hand.

He put the tools away and came towards the house with his stomach churning. He waited for a while, allowing the wind to push him this way and that, feeling the first little spots of rain against the brim of his hat. And after what seemed like another eternity, the scullery door finally swung open and Billy and Jeannie came out, hand in hand, and slowly, almost reluctantly, walked towards him, their faces solemn, scared.

When they were close enough they stopped, and Billy said, 'Mrs Price said you wanted to talk to us.'

Harry nodded, having no real idea what he was going to say. The rain began to fall a little heavier then. It pattered against the trees, drummed gently on the roof of the shelter behind him.

'How was school?' he asked.

Billy shrugged. 'All right.'

'I did some painting,' Jeannie said, and held up her fingers so that he could see the little spots of green and yellow that still clung stubbornly to her nails.

'Lovely,' he said awkwardly. Then, 'I've got something to tell you two, and it's not going to be any easier for me to say it than it is for you to hear it. But I'll just get it said, and then we'll, uh, take it from there, shall we?'

The children looked up at him as if they were about to receive a punishment. Perhaps in a way they were.

'Billy,' he said. 'Jeannie.'

Silence.

Then–

'I'm your dad.'

Neither child moved. Billy, in particular, sat as still as a statue. Outside, thunder growled ominously, and the rain came down harder, hitting the roof more like hailstones.

'You're lyin',' Billy said at last. 'My dad's a spy. He works for Neville Chamberlain.'

'I'm not lying to you, son,' Harry said softly. 'I just … it's been so long, I didn't know how…'

'Your name's not Curtis,' said Jeannie.

'It *is*. Gordon … that's my middle name.'

'It's not!' snapped Billy. 'You're lyin'!'

'Look, all I ask is that you hear me out,' said Harry. 'Let me explain–'

'No!' cried Billy, and Jeannie, not properly understanding what was going on, started to cry. 'Mum said my dad went away because he didn't want to be with us anymore!'

'That's not true–'

'Well, that's what she said! Why did she say that if it wasn't true?'

Harry reached for the boy but Billy shook him off, leapt up from the stool and squeezed past him to get to the door. 'Get away from me!' he screamed. 'You're not my dad!'

He tore the door open. The wind immediately lashed at him, throwing rain into his face so that it mixed with his tears.

In the next moment he was gone.

'*Billy–!*'

Harry got up, limped to the door just in time to see Billy disappear through the gate at the side of the house, already soaked to the skin. He caught sight of Beryl watching from the scullery door, shrugged like a little boy lost himself and gestured that he needed help with Jeannie, who was now sobbing hard.

Beryl hurried up the path, the rain plastering her hair flat. She called, 'I'll see to her!'

Harry nodded and went after Billy, moving as quickly as his bad leg would allow.

He reached the gate, shoved through it, staggered out into the lane, looked right, then left–

A flash of lightning lit the sky, and by its searing white glow he saw the boy racing away, splashing through puddles.

'Billy!' he yelled. *'Billy!'*

But if the boy heard him, he gave no indication of it.

His face screwed into an agony of despair, Harry broke into a shambling trot after the boy. This wasn't the way it was supposed to be, and it wouldn't have been this way at all, if only the Home Office hadn't sent Beryl that damned letter! But once Beryl and Evelyn knew the truth, there could be no more deception, and ready or not, he'd had no choice but to tell them the way of it all.

He ran as far as he could, but it wasn't anywhere near as far as he would have liked. Eventually he had to revert to his ungainly hobble, his guts wound tight, his emotions running higher than they ever had before.

His only consolation now was that he knew where he would find Billy. There was only one place he would go at a time like this – to the abbey ruins.

Awkwardly he clambered over the stile, dragging his useless leg behind him. Another lightning strike lit the abbey, and it stood before him, a silhouette at once both majestic and sinister, set against a dark and turbulent sky.

He'd been here before, of course, several times: had come to enjoy the peace and seclusion it gave a man to make sense of his life and decide how best he should live it. He'd had no way of knowing then that Billy had also found it a place of comfort, until the day he'd watched the boy from afar when he'd been hurting over some upset or other, bleeding from a grazed knee and exhausted by emotion.

He'd wanted to go to him then but had held back for fear of just this reaction.

Then the lad had fallen asleep and he'd crept closer, and as he'd looked down he'd seen himself in the boy: the same eyes, the same mouth, the same shade of thick brown hair. His lips had tightened, his Adam's apple had worked, and he'd wanted to wake the lad and tell him the truth, until he gave the matter more thought and suddenly saw himself through Billy's eyes.

Face it: he was a crippled scarecrow of a man, a man who'd been broken by life. Was that what *any* lad would want for a father?

He doubted it.

So he'd decided to get to know the boy first as a stranger, and more importantly let the boy get to know *him*, and when the bond between them grew strong enough – if it *ever* grew strong enough – then he would tell him the truth.

But Billy had taken more winning over than he'd dreamed, and he'd never quite understood why the boy had taken such an instant dislike to him. The idea that Billy hated him now was more than he could stand, and if nothing else he felt he had to set things right between them.

Even if the boy didn't want anything more to do with him, he had to do *that* much, at least.

Chapter Twenty-One

Acceptance

Billy hunkered down behind the fallen spire and let the rain lash at him. He'd found comfort here on so many occasions in the past, but this time it eluded him.

So what?

What did *anything* matter, now? Harry had said he was their father, but for reasons of his own he'd lied to them all this time, pretended to be someone else. Why, then, come clean *now?* As far as he could see, there was only one reason. Harry was going to take them away from Mrs Price, and Edward and Peter, and Mrs Murray and Little Asham. He was going to take them back to London, and neither he nor Jeannie would ever see any of this or any of these people ever again.

That alone was bad enough. But Billy knew only too well what must come after that. It was inevitable, a case of history repeating itself.

Harry would soon get fed up with them again, as he had before. Mum had told them so. He'd gotten fed up with them then and decided he didn't want to be with them anymore, and so he'd abandoned them.

He'd abandon them again, sooner or later.

Billy sniffed and shook his head. Rain dripped from his hair down across his eyebrows, and he started to shiver.

The worst of it was that he'd taken to the man from the first. Perhaps he'd seen something of himself in Harry and just didn't recognise it. Whatever it was, he'd liked him, and yet he'd been *afraid* to like him. Like someone too much and sooner or later they leave you, the way Dad – Harry – had, the way Mum had by choosing Uncle George over them.

That's why he'd decided that the only way to stop Harry from leaving them was to *not* like him too much. But now he was going to take them away from every*thing* and every*one* else, and there was nothing they could do to stop him.

A shadow fell across him and his head snapped up just as Harry came around the corner of the ruined tower and bent to shelter beside him. Both were soaked through, their clothes dark, their faces pebbled with rainwater. Thunder grumbled in the distance, and a gust of wind swatted them with an invisible fist.

They looked at each other for a long moment, and for each one it was more like looking into a mirror. No wonder Beryl had been so sure she'd seen Harry somewhere else. She had – in his son.

'Billy,' Harry said quietly, and shook his head. 'There's so much I need to tell you.'

'I don't want to hear it,' snapped Billy.

'Well, you're *going* to hear it,' said Harry. He snaked an arm around Billy's shoulders, and though the boy tried to shrug out of his hold, he didn't try as hard as he might have. Harry drew him close, felt him shivering and gave him a squeeze. 'I *am* your father, you know. And I realise I must be a bit of a disappointment. I mean, I'm sure you thought I was a lot more than I actually *am.*'

Billy said nothing.

'Billy,' Harry continued, 'I came here to *find* you, son. You and Jeannie. You might not believe it, but I want us to be together again. I want that with all my heart. Lord knows, we've spent enough years *apart.*'

'Yeah,' said Billy, venomously. 'Because *you* walked out on us!'

The accusation stung. 'Is that what your mother told you?'

Billy looked away from him. 'She said you didn't want to be with us anymore.'

'Well, that's not true,' Harry insisted. 'Something happened, and I had to go away, and it just about *killed* me to be parted from you two.'

He glanced up at the angry sky, where the clouds bulked together and turned late afternoon into twilight.

'Would you like me to tell you that you were right, that I *am* a spy working for Neville Chamberlain, and that all this time I've been spying on the Nazis?' he asked. 'Would that make everything right between us? Or would you prefer to hear the *truth?*'

The boy spared him another fleeting glance. 'The truth,' he said after a long moment.

Harry nodded. 'All right.'

He sighed.

'The truth is that I did something I shouldn't have done, and I went to prison for it.'

Billy absorbed that in silence. 'It must have been something very bad,' he said in a small voice.

'It could've been worse, but it was bad enough,' replied Harry. 'And I'm not making any excuses for what I did. I got in with a bad crowd, and I *knew* they were bad, but I suppose it made me feel good to be one of the boys. You know, *important*. Besides, we needed money, your mother and I. We *always* needed money. And running with a crowd like that ... well, there was always good money to be made.'

Billy was silent.

'The truth was, they were small-time jack-the-lads, these friends of mine. But then they got it into their heads to do over this jeweller's, see. Smash and grab, in broad daylight. And they wanted me to drive the getaway car.

'The minute I agreed, I regretted it. But once I'd given my word I couldn't let them down or they'd have had my hide.'

He laughed shortly and without humour. 'God, I was as sick as a dog the morning of the job, so nervous I could hardly stop my hands from shaking. But we picked up the car – one of the lads had stolen it the night before – and I drove us to the jeweller's. The boys jumped out and threw a brick at the shop window, and it smashed and they started snatching up as much as they could carry.

'But someone must have talked, because all of a sudden there were coppers everywhere. I panicked, tried to make a getaway but only made it as far as the end of the road. A police car came around the corner and cut me off, and I swerved to avoid it and hit a post box instead. I broke my leg and did something to my hip.

'Next thing I knew I was in a hospital bed with a police guard. Turns out they got every one of them. They charged me with conspiracy to steal and gave me eight years.'

He looked Billy in the face. '*That's* where your old dad's been all that time, son,' he said. 'In prison. And do you know something?'

'What?' Billy asked grudgingly.

'The worst part of it was not getting the chance to see you and Jeannie grow up. If I'd known that at the start, I wouldn't have gone within a hundred miles of that shop.'

Billy frowned. 'Eight years,' he said suddenly. 'You said eight years.'

Harry nodded. 'Yes. But after your mother ... after your mother passed away, they let me out early on what they call compassionate grounds. They knew you and Jeannie would need looking after, see.

'Anyway, I went to your school, and they told me that you'd both been evacuated here, so I came down and got myself a room in Fenby and tried to figure out how to come back into your life so that it wouldn't be such a shock.' He shook his head miserably. 'I didn't make a very good job of it, did I?'

He shook his head, let go a heavy sigh. 'It's funny, though, how things turn out. I came down here to figure out a way to come back into your life, but our paths started crossing before I was ready.' He laughed suddenly. 'Remember that murky day when you and your friends thought you saw a ghost?'

Billy wiped at his eyes. 'Was that you?'

'Gave you a right old scare, didn't I? Not that I meant to. It's just that I always seemed to be drawn here. It was peaceful, somewhere a man could be himself.'

A new thought occurred to Billy. 'I found a cigarette card just over there. Was that yours?'

'I can't think who else's.'

The rain had slackened to a light drizzle, and the clouds were starting to break apart to reveal the bluer sky beyond. Harry said, 'I know this is a lot to take in, son. I wouldn't have told you the truth even now, but Mrs Price received a letter from the Home Office this morning, telling her that I'd been given early release. She saw my full name on the letter and told me I couldn't keep pretending. She was probably right.'

'But why did Mum tell us you didn't want to be with us anymore?'

'I don't know. She had to tell you *something*, I suppose. And she was furious with me, because I'd got myself caught and wrecked *all* our lives.

'Anyway, it's done now. I don't know what else to say, except that I'm sorry, and that I love you. I never *stopped* loving you. You and Jeannie were all I thought about through all those years. The thought of seeing you again and doing whatever I could to make it up to you, they were the things that kept me going.

'But it's up to you what happens next, son. Will you give me a chance? Will you at least *think* about giving me a chance?'

Billy dug deep into his pocket. His fingers closed around his mother's wedding ring. 'We'd better go back,' he muttered.

Harry stayed over that night, and the following day Beryl kept Billy and Jeannie home from school in the hope that they would spend some time getting to know their father all over again. Jeannie didn't seem to have any real problem. She'd taken to Harry from the start, and was now tickled pink to discover that he was her daddy.

Billy, however, was a different matter.

Beryl assured Harry that he would come round in time, but Harry wasn't so sure. He suggested it might be best if he left Beryl's employment, but neither she nor Evelyn would hear of it. Besides, with winter fast approaching, there was still plenty to do.

So he arrived as usual first thing every morning and worked right through till dusk, thinning the trees and clearing the bracken, taking his breaks in the shelter and waiting, always waiting, for Billy to come round.

It was almost the end of November now, and still difficult to believe that there was a war on. In fact, some people had taken to calling it the 'Phoney War' because with one or two exceptions, all anyone seemed to have done so far was hang around and wait. Some of the evacuees, including Jeannie's best friend Ann, had even returned home.

Evelyn had decided to stay on with Peter at Holly Cottage. It was less than three months now until the baby arrived, so it was probably best if they stayed where they were.

On one particular morning, Peter received a letter from his father. It was only a short note, but the boy was over the moon.

Billy, still keeping mostly to himself, sensed Peter's excitement and remembered all the times he'd wished he could have received a letter from his own father. He thought about Harry almost all the time, wondering who had been telling the truth, his mother or his father? He was reluctant to trust Harry and leave himself open to that dreadful sense of loss when the man decided to leave them all over again.

And yet he was inclined to believe Harry when he said he wanted to look after them, that thoughts of he and Jeannie had kept him going throughout the years in prison.

And look how he was with Jeannie. Too young to know any different, the girl idolized him, already called him 'Dad' without a second thought, and he certainly seemed to dote on her.

Secretly Billy wished he could set aside all his doubts and uncertainties and enjoy some of that affection himself. But he just didn't feel able to. He was sure that the minute he let his guard down, Harry would show his true colours and vanish from their lives again.

In any case, would that be so bad? Life would get back to normal if Harry were to leave.

He wanted to feel happy at such a prospect, and yet it made him feel anything *but*. He liked Harry. He had *always* liked Harry, even when he suspected that he was a German spy!

Then what was he to do?

He pondered the problem long and hard

for the rest of that week, and at the end of it admitted to himself that it was harder to hate Harry than it would be to love him.

Whether he liked it or not, he *had* to take a chance, to set aside all his doubts and fears and dare to trust his father not to let him down.

Harry was sawing at a branch when Billy entered the orchard. Edward and Peter were playing *Happy Families* in Edward's room, and Jeannie was helping Beryl make some fairy cakes.

Harry didn't see the boy until he was standing right beside him. Then he raised his eyebrows in surprise and, setting his saw aside, said cautiously, 'Hello, Billy. You all right, son?'

Billy nodded. He looked very serious. 'I, ah...' he began.

Harry looked down at him, aching for his acceptance. 'Yes?' he prompted.

'I just wanted to give you this,' said Billy.

He handed over the sheet of paper he'd been holding behind his back, then turned and started to walk away.

Harry looked down at it. It was the drawing the boy had done weeks before, of him at work on the shelter. In one corner the boy had written:

For Dad,
With love from
Billy

For one split second the breath caught in Harry's throat and his head dropped briefly. Then he turned and called, 'Billy!'

Billy looked back at him.

'Thank you, son.'

Billy shrugged. 'That's all right.'

'I'll never let you down again,' Harry said quietly. 'I promise.'

Billy looked at him and muttered, 'I know.'

Some new understanding seemed to grow between them in that moment, and when Harry finally dared to open his arms, there was no hesitation: Billy rushed straight into them, and they held each other tight.

Harry said, 'I *do* love you, Billy.'

Billy nodded. 'And I love you too,' he said, adding in a whisper, '...*Dad.*'

Epilogue

Thump!

A kit bag landed squarely in the middle of Little Asham's station platform and its owner, a medium-sized man dressed in the uniform of the Royal Engineers, jumped down from the train, tugged at the waist-band of his tunic and brushed himself down.

It had been a long, rushed journey and he was happy to have finally reached his destination. He walked out onto the lane, the gravel crunching noisily under his sturdy army boots.

It was Christmas Eve, and he'd been lucky to get leave: lucky also to jump aboard a troop ship that was just about to leave France for Dover.

As he left the station behind him he whistled a few bars of *Good King Wenceslas,* hoping that he might spot someone from whom to ask directions.

Up ahead, a little girl was skipping towards him, a man with a cane, and a young boy, walking along side by side a few yards behind her. He grinned briefly. The boy reminded him of his son.

As the girl drew level, he said, 'Excuse me, princess. Do you happen to know where Holly Cottage is?'

The little girl looked surprised. 'That's where *we're* going!' she answered.

By this time, the man and boy had caught up, and were treating the newcomer to a curious appraisal.

'You're not Tom Murray, by any chance?' asked the man. 'Evelyn's husband?'

'Guilty as charged!' chuckled the soldier.

'Well, I'll be blowed! I'm Harry! Harry

Curtis! This is my son, Billy, and my little girl, Jeannie. They were evacuated with Peter!'

Tom offered a hand. 'Pleased to meet you, Harry.'

'Come on, the cottage is only up here,' Harry said, as they began to walk up the lane. 'There are two people up there who're going to be very happy to see you,' he predicted.

'Are they all well?' Tom asked anxiously.

'Oh, they're fine, just fine.'

'I didn't get a chance to let Eve know I was coming. It was a last-minute thing, you know.' He ruffled Billy's hair. 'Peter's told me all about your adventures,' he said. And to Harry he added, 'I can't tell you what it's like to get those letters!'

'I can imagine,' said Harry, as they walked up the path and round to the side gate. 'We're living in a little rented cottage by the village green ourselves,' he explained.

As they slipped into the scullery, Harry put a finger to his lips. 'Not a word, you two. You wait here a minute, Tom.'

Harry, Billy and Jeannie went through to the kitchen. The room had been warmed by the range and smelled of freshly-baked mince pies. Edward and Peter were sitting at the table, playing *Snap*. Beryl was fussing over the enormous turkey she'd bought from Mrs Norman. Evelyn sat by the range, feeding tidbits to a brown and white Jack Russell puppy called Snowflake – Edward's main Christmas present for that year.

'Hello, strangers!' greeted Beryl. 'Come and sit yourself down, Harry. You look like you could do with a bit of a warm-up!'

Jeannie made a bee-line for the puppy, her earlier fear of dogs suddenly forgotten. Snowflake threw himself at her, his tiny tail a blur.

Just as he sat down, Harry snapped his fingers. 'Oh, by the way, Evelyn. I met someone on the way down here who *knows* you.'

Evelyn frowned. 'Knows *me?*' she asked.

'Yes. You and Peter both.'

Right on cue, the scullery door swung open and Tom came inside. *'Ta-da!'*

Peter dropped his cards and his eyes went wide. *'Dad!'* he cried, and leapt off his chair to fling himself into his father's arms.

Snowflake started yapping.

Evelyn looked stunned to see Tom there. Her eyes misted, her lips quivered. 'Oh, Tom…' she finally managed.

She got up with effort and crossed to him, and they embraced. The moment was thick with emotion, and Billy watched on with excitement shining in his eyes.

'Dad,' he said, hoisting himself up into his father's lap.

Harry looked at him. 'What is it, son?'

'This is goin' to be the best Christmas ever, innit?'

Harry pulled him close. 'No,' he said. 'It's going to be even *better* than that.'

This Large Print Book, for people
who cannot read normal print,
is published under the auspices of

THE ULVERSCROFT FOUNDATION

... we hope you have enjoyed this book.
Please think for a moment about those
who have worse eyesight than you ...
and are unable to even read or enjoy
Large Print without great difficulty.

You can help them by sending a
donation, large or small, to:

**The Ulverscroft Foundation,
1, The Green, Bradgate Road,
Anstey, Leicestershire, LE7 7FU,
England.**
or request a copy of our brochure for
more details.

The Foundation will use all donations
to assist those people who are visually
impaired and need special attention
with medical research, diagnosis
and treatment.

Thank you very much for your help.